TAKING ON THE ORLANDO MOB
The Funny Detective – Volume 1

David Berardelli

TAKING ON THE ORLANDO MOB
The Funny Detective – Volume 1

FICTION4ALL

Chapter 1

I don't know why I should be surprised by anything anymore.

When you've been operating a small one-man detective agency on Orange Avenue in the heart of downtown Orlando for five years, you see a lot of weird things. Florida is the Mecca for weird, Orlando the epitome for super weird. Adults sporting Goofy masks and Mickey ears wandering around as if Goofy masks and Mickey ears were the latest in high fashion. Motorists getting out of their cars at the scene of an accident and approaching a traffic cop for directions. Elderly Asian men just off the plane trying to drive and read American road signs in heavy afternoon traffic. Turban-headed men in suits running red lights, then jumping out of their rented Cadillac to scream in their native language at the motorist they've just T-boned.

I've been living here for twenty years, have seen just about every mindless thing there is to see and keep hoping that what I *haven't* seen won't get me killed or maimed.

But even though I'm a top-notch private eye and always on my guard, I still wasn't prepared for what would happen that evening.

***

Earlier that afternoon, a tall, broad-shouldered woman bulled her way into my office.

She said her name was Sandra Brandon. She had a low voice and a hard femininity that would scare off most guys and have them covering their crotches while running for cover. Her thick brown hair reached her shoulders. She wore her clothes well and didn't overdo her makeup. But nice hair, a great figure and tasteful makeup don't matter much when you suspect the woman can easily knock you on your ass.

"My ex-husband's name is Don," she said, sitting down in the chair facing my desk. "He's big, strong and good-looking. He's also a pig."

"A pig?" I asked, more for verification than any sort of hearing disability.

"Pig. P-I-G."

I wanted to thank her for spelling it for me. Sometimes I give people the impression I'm dim-witted. This is because I usually have too many things going on in my head and it makes me uncomfortable. As a result, I tend to appear confused and oftentimes constipated when I should really be showing off my customary wit and charm.

"Does he walk upright?" I asked. "Or on all fours, like so many other pigs we know and love?"

She was not amused. I had a feeling even my legendary captivating humor wouldn't be enough to get her to crack her face. Some women just don't understand the need for levity when they're furious. My ex-wife Phil was a perfect example.

"Do you always try to be funny?" she asked.

"Sometimes I actually achieve it," I said proudly.

"This must be a slow day for you."

"Depends on the crowd."

6

She pulled a small glossy photo from her purse and handed it over. I laid it carefully on my desk blotter in front of the silver pen and pencil set Phil gave me for my thirty-fifth birthday, just four short years ago.

Sandra was right. Don was a looker in a "bad-boy" sort of way. He could easily be a contestant on Extreme Fighting--not exactly the sort of quarry I prefer for my usual assignments. But it always made me wonder why so many women fell for such guys when bad boys wanted a quick roll in the hay, some booze, drugs, and a place to crash. Pursuing a deep commitment or a lasting relationship was not high on their short list of priorities.

But what did I know? I was only one guy and, according to Phil--as well as several other women I'd known in my skirt-chasing career--I had no idea what it took to press a woman's buttons.

"That was taken about a year ago." Sandra Brandon snapped her purse shut. "He might have shaved off the goatee. He's always shaving something off or growing something else."

That was a perfect lead-in for a zinger, but the vibes in the room told me to leave it be. I was heart-broken but forced myself to forget about it. There would be other joke-making opportunities.

"What's he done?" I asked.

"He knocked me up. Then he made tracks. I told you he's a pig, didn't I?"

"I vaguely remember you mentioning that, yes."

Sandra Brandon sat back and crossed her arms in front of her.

"How much back child support are we talking about?"

"Three years, so far. Bastard's supposed to pay me six hundred a month. Know what that comes out to?"

"A handsome chunk of change."

She grunted.

I wanted to ask if her grunt meant agreement or just a little residual reflux from sharing the sheets with a pig.

"What are your rates? Someone told me you're pretty cheap."

I hated it when people didn't get their facts right. "I prefer to say I'm more reasonable than my competition."

"Whatever." She opened her purse again and pulled out a thick wad. The top bill was a hundred. Unless everything else underneath was a one or a five, she could have an easy ten grand in those hot little manicured hands. It made me wonder why she needed child support money in the first place. But I was never one to cause trouble. "How much will a grand get me?"

"Four days of my complete, undying cooperation." I hoped she'd just hand me the wad. I'd promise to give her back what I didn't need when the assignment was finished.

She carefully peeled off ten bills and dropped them on my desk.

***

According to Sandra, Don Brandon spent a lot of his time in the dirtiest tittie bars on South Orange Blossom Trail.

One of Brandon's favorite haunts, Kelsey's Bar in downtown Orlando, makes strong drinks for guys wanting to get drunk fast. You can also buy drugs and find a fairly cheap hooker while you're there.

Since Kelsey's wasn't far from my office, I decided to start my search there.

I wasn't wild about going there, but since I didn't have any other leads, I didn't have much choice. This area was popular for vagrants, hookers and druggies. Not exactly the sort you wanted to meet at night--especially when you were alone.

But when someone just paid you enough money to make your rent for the next few weeks, you forced yourself to ignore a little minor discomfort.

A shot of Jack's would also have helped start the ball rolling.

My supply in the flask had run out just before lunch. I hadn't had time to put in my usual grand appearance at the local liquor store yet. I still had a splash or two left in the bottle in the bottom drawer of my desk and a quarter-bottle back at the apartment.

It would have to wait.

Except for the flashing neon, the aging brick building reminded me of one of those giant sea creatures living at the bottom of the ocean. The kind that doesn't move until some unsuspecting prey gets a little too close to its huge mouth.

I cautiously approached, keeping alert so I couldn't be jumped by someone hiding between the parked cars lining the curb. My penlight lay nestled in my jacket pocket, ready to douse the darkness. I'd only flick it on in an emergency. You never knew who was hiding between parked cars. I figured if someone was hiding between cars, he wouldn't appreciate a sudden jolt of blinding light in his eyes. I'm a sleuth, not a skull-crusher. I don't mind finding out a few things for people, but I'm definitely not the type to risk broken bones for some walking-around money.

What good is walking-around money if your legs are broken?

As an independent sleuth, I don't have the money to buy medical insurance. Even if I did, it would take much too long to find a carrier who wouldn't laugh hysterically when I told him my profession. Insurance agents are funny about such things.

As usual, I had my little Bersa .380 with me. It makes me feel more confident even though I've never had to use it. I hoped I never would.

I'm a lousy shot. I have this irritating habit of shaking whenever I point my gun at someone. When you're shaking, hitting your target is a real challenge. And when you aim, you'd better have the balls to pull the trigger. I just can't put myself into that mindset, and whenever I try, I shake. I figure that if I spend enough time at the shooting range, the experience will improve my aim and give me the confidence I need. It hasn't worked yet but I'm still hopeful.

Kelsey's throbbed louder as I approached. It hadn't sucked anyone in since I'd gotten out of my car but I remained cautious anyway. The windows blazed with light. Even outside you could hear Elvis in his heyday bellowing from the juke.

I always thought the name Kelsey ironic. It's right out of *All in the Family*. But that's where the similarity ends. I'd been here once before, and if there was any humor floating around, I hadn't picked the right day to see it. Truckers, dock workers, fishermen and laborers came here after work, some to get drunk, others to get drunk and fight, still others to get drunk and proposition the hookers. They weren't what you'd call a humorous bunch. I was never too fond of placing myself at the mercy of a roomful of drunken blue-collar testosterone. You could get seriously hurt.

I paused before going inside. The best and safest thing a detective can do is have his subject's face clear in his head. When you have a clear picture, you can scan the perimeter quickly and make tracks if things get hairy. Brandon was six-one, weighed in at around two-ten, shaved his head and looked like someone you'd expect to see on a Post Office wall or escorting an MTV diva to an awards ceremony. He'd been in the Navy, did some boxing--which explained the broken nose--was a sucker for boilermakers and cheap hookers and thought nothing of snorting his paycheck.

11

He was definitely bad news. He probably wouldn't appreciate knowing the lovely Sandra had just paid an expert sleuth a thousand bucks to track him down.

My pulse hastening, I carefully pushed open the door and hoped it wouldn't swallow me whole.

The room was deafening, this time with Garth Brooks. Some intense arm-wrestling went on at a couple of tables, but mostly everyone just drank and stared glossy-eyed at the three plump hookers sitting at the bar in their bright spandex outfits.

A quick scan revealed no sign of Brandon.

Rule Number One for finding someone in a crowded bar: Always approach the barman first. He sees and knows everything and could care less who is cheating on who or dodging child support payments. Slipping him a ten-spot always gets you somewhere, and when you use your charm as an added bonus, you can't lose.

"Whaddya have?" He was around thirty and an inch or so taller than me--which put him at around six-one. He hauled around a pair of muscular arms covered with tattoos and kept his black mustache trimmed and waxed at the ends. His coal-black eyes were dead-steady. He seemed upset. He was probably waiting for the right CEO position to open up and forced to work in this loud, dirty place until his Big Moment arrived.

"Seen this guy?" I placed the photo carefully on a dry section of counter.

He picked up a glass and polished it with the white cloth dangling from his belt. He'd either had his fill of the professional sleuth's Rule Number One in the past or wasn't in the mood to be helpful. Instead of looking at the photo, he stared at me. He didn't appear to be gay, but you never knew nowadays. Prison oozed with homosexuals who looked like Conan the Barbarian on steroids. Also, a lot of guys went into prison straight and ended up gay or bi. I tossed him a pleasant grin but it didn't go very far. A ten-spot would have been better. I pulled one from my pants pocket and slid it over.

He didn't touch it.

"I take it that's a no." I pocketed the photo but left the ten-spot. He was probably sizing me up to see if I'd leave the bill even though he wasn't going to be cooperative. I decided to keep him guessing. I left it there.

Someone tapped me on the shoulder. A little bald-headed guy perched on the barstool to my right grinned at me. He was probably around fifty or so, but I've always had trouble determining a bald man's age. He could've been forty or even younger.

"Back there!" he yelled over the throbbing juke. He stabbed a thumb at the lighted doorway marked *BABES* and *BULLS*.

I tried a gamble. "Men's room?"

He shrugged. "Something going on down that hall." He picked up his beer and had a big slug.

"What's going on?"

"Can't see much from here."

"I can see that."

"See what?"

"I can see that you can't see much from here."

"You're good." He had another slug of beer.

"You need to tell my ex-wife, but she probably won't believe you."

I left him scratching his bald head and slipped through the open doorway. The well-lit carpeted hall went past the restrooms to a door marked *OFFICE*. A sliver of yellow light showing beneath the door told me something was going on inside.

Procedure in this case? Act innocent. You don't know what's happening and you don't know anyone. If something illegal is going on, avoid all eye contact and get out fast. If it's just a high-stakes poker game, the situation will be much less stressful. Say, *Oops--sorry, guys, thought this was where Lila told me to meet her*. Lila was always a good name to use. Lila or Amber. That'll usually get them wondering if they know anyone by that name. Hopefully, one or more of them won't actually be involved with someone named Lila or Amber. If so, then you're in *seriously* bad shape. If not, someone will invariably say, *Can't you read*? Or, if you're *really* lucky, *Poker, fella? A buck gets you in*. Then you can always successfully bow out with any number of stupid lines.

Stupid can get you out of a *lot* of trouble.

So can a snappy line.

I reached for the doorknob.

Locked. *Damn . . .*

The men's room, then.

The room reeked of urine, mold and bleach. The closed window, sealed shut with several layers of paint, kept the stench contained. A naked light

14

bulb hung from a long, frayed cord. The filmy mirror barely showed my reflection. A beat-up white trash can shoved against the grimy tile wall stood beside the stained sink. Crumpled towels littered the soiled linoleum. The urinal looked like it hadn't been cleaned since the Reagan years.

The only feature in the room pleasing to the eye was the slender brunette staring curiously at me from the open stall.

She was about twenty-five, with long dark hair, large dark almond eyes, high cheekbones, and full lips. She was two or three inches shorter than me and dressed in tight jeans, a red tee shirt, tan jacket and tennis shoes. Small gold necklaces glittered beneath her collarbone. Her face sure was nice. Too nice for a dirty men's room.

This is where protocol turns vague, and discretion takes over. Since I was never very good at discretion, I always managed to get into trouble in tight situations. I'm looking for a guy, someone tells me to come back here and now I'm facing a good-looking chick in a foul-smelling men's room.

My lack of discretion urged me to say something witty, like, "Pizza delivery" or "We've got to stop meeting like this." But since I was nervous about being here in the first place, I knew my usual dry casual wit would be lacking. I decided to be cool and ease as gracefully as possible out of the room. Then I could take my chances with the little bald-headed guy who told me to come back here.

"Hi," I said, oozing my usual charisma.

She nodded but said nothing.

Since I obviously hadn't scored any points with my charisma, I decided to sound clever. "Could've sworn this was the men's room."

She just kept staring at me.

"This *is* the men's room, isn't it?"

Still no reply.

I decided to break the ice with a little humor. "I didn't by any chance switch genders while I wasn't looking, did I?" I raised and lowered my brows in my best Groucho Marx.

That didn't faze her. Maybe she was too young for Groucho. I'd try Harpo, but I'd need a harp and a bicycle horn. With Chico, I'd need a piano and a bad Italian accent. I never could quite figure out Zeppo and was even less sure about Gummo.

"Is one of us . . . lost?" I tried to be subtle and informative at the same time.

Still no response.

She obviously didn't care too much for humor, cleverness, wit or charisma. Not even being subtle or informative. What was left?

I was a private detective. I was supposed to be calm, calculated and professional. Equipped to handle every type of weird situation.

And most of all, unshakable.

Debonair, perhaps. That wasn't exactly one of my better qualities, but I could wing it. When you're calm, calculated and professional, you can do just about anything.

This situation called for the Cary Grant touch. I was about to break her down with one of his best lines from *Philadelphia Story* when she whispered, "You really need to get out of here."

"No problem," I whispered back. In my own voice, of course, since I didn't want to confuse her. I gave her a sly wink. Sort of a buddy-buddy type thing to put her at ease.

"I'm serious. Someone's about to come in here, looking for you."

I wanted to ask how she knew but all I could manage was, "It's okay. I'm a private eye. I'm used to shit like this."

Voices out in the hall.

The bathroom door swung open. The juke increased in volume, this time with Elvis from his Vegas days.

I didn't have time to turn to see who it was before something heavy and hard cracked me on the back of the head.

Chapter 2

My doctor was large, white-haired, and reeked of Aqua Velva and cigarettes.

His thick-rimmed glasses were balanced on the tip of his fleshy red nose. He was whistling while applying the dressing to the back of my head. At first I thought it was *Help Me, Rhonda*. But then it sounded more like *Wipeout*. He was obviously tone-deaf, but I didn't want to make any comment. You didn't want to irritate someone stitching up your head. It just isn't very bright.

Just then, his thumb touched something sensitive and I cringed at the stab of heat jolting mercilessly down my neck.

"Hurt?" he asked.

"Naw, I think you just found my G-spot."

"We don't have those."

"You sure?"

"Reasonably."

"Good thing. We have enough problems."

"You're lucky, though."

"Because I don't have a G-spot?"

"Because you've got a hard head."

"Thanks."

"You're welcome."

"Ever watch *House*?"

"Once or twice."

"Not all the time?"

"I'm usually here most nights, stitching up idiots like you who like to get into bar fights."

18

"You've got him down pat."

"He's my hero," he said flatly.

"You've really got helluva bedside manner."

"Yeah, they keep telling me I need to work on that." He shuffled over to the sink. "One of these days, maybe." He pulled off his gloves, dropped them in the trash and washed his hands.

The slim, dark-haired nurse cleaned up the mess on the dressing table. She was Asian, around thirty-five and, judging by the rock on her finger, married to someone who thought she was a first-class investment.

A tall, broad-shouldered cop came in. His nametag said *ROLLINS*. He was around forty, had a toothpick stuck in the left corner of his mouth and acted just as bored and as irritable as most of the other cops I knew. He held a notepad and pen in his left hand. "You're him?"

"*Him*? As opposed to *her*?" I looked down at my lap. "Last I checked."

"Deacon."

"Guilty."

"You run that agency on Orange? North of Michigan?"

"That's my turf."

"You went to school with Ozzie Taylor, right?"

"Ozzie still around?"

"He's DEA now. What happened?"

"To Ozzie?"

"To you."

I shrugged. "I got rolled."

19

"They said they found you outside the Courthouse on Hughey, the back of your head split open."

"I wouldn't know."

"What were you doing?"

"Lying there with my head split open, apparently."

"So you got rolled and whoever did it dumped you there?"

"Since I was unconscious at the time, anything's possible."

"I take it you were on a case?"

"It started out that way but went south really fast."

"I'll bet I know what happened."

"You were there?"

"Didn't have to be."

"I give up. What happened?"

"You turned your back on the wrong guy."

I gave a low whistle. "You're good."

"Some things come naturally. Did you check to see if you're missing anything?"

"Since when?"

"Since they brought you in."

"Actually, I've been much too busy grinding my teeth from having my brains shoved back inside my skull."

"No biggie," the doc said, still washing his hands. "Only took a few seconds."

"Thanks for the evaluation," I said.

The doc shrugged. "Don't worry. I'm pretty sure I got everything."

"So I guess you don't remember being brought in," Rollins said.

"You really *are* good."

"Try being serious once in a while. I'm trying to decide how to treat this case."

"All I remember is a dynamite dream featuring yours truly swapping spit with a half-naked Naomi Watts."

He nodded. "Good dream."

"You got *that* right. You can't imagine how pissed I was when I opened my eyes and saw Mister Personality over there with his needle and thread, salivating all over his scrub shirt."

"That would rile me, too."

"Life is filled with disappointments. And since you asked, I'm missing my wallet and gun."

He began scribbling, then stopped. A wide grin drifted across his pockmarked features. "You that guy, came out to the shooting range the other day and--"

"That was me." How come cops didn't forget certain things like normal human beings?

"That was *true*? You really shot out the lights?"

My gun was pointed toward the ceiling when I was changing clips. I pinched a wedge of palm flesh with the clip, jerked and accidentally pulled the trigger. "My gun . . . misfired."

"But the lights . . . they're--"

"Overhead. Yeah. I know. Got any idea how many people have reminded me of that?"

He stifled a snicker and nearly choked on his toothpick. I wanted to help it along but figured he might forget about my embarrassing shooting accident if I reminded him why he was here. "Like I said, I'm missing my wallet and gun."

"You'll have to come in and fill out a report. What kind of gun?"

"A three-eighty Bersa."

Rollins nodded. "Poor man's Walther."

"Two hundred bucks as opposed to over a grand and it shoots just as good. And it doesn't jam."

"Really?" He blinked.

"Even a bad shot like me doesn't want his gun to jam."

His grin came back. "I'd think you'd *want* it to jam before--"

"Maybe I *wanted* to shoot out the damned lights." Rollins was really annoying--even for a cop.

"Now why would you want to do something like *that*?"

"The glare was too much. It affected my aim."

"You're not serious."

"Just as serious as your contribution to this conversation."

This time he couldn't hold back the laughter. I wanted to shove his notepad and pen up his ass. "You having fun?" I asked.

He finally got it under control. He wiped his eyes and sniffed. "Where'd you start out?" he asked. "Before you were rolled."

"Kelsey's."

He frowned. The toothpick had shifted to the right side of his mouth. "That area's pretty rough."

"Really? Thanks."

"What were you doing there?"

"Tracking down a deadbeat dad."

"Find him?"

"I think he found me."

Rollins shut the notepad. "Don't forget to come in and fill out that report. Within the next twenty-four hours would be great. You got the serial number for the Bersa?"

"Somewhere."

"Don't forget to get in touch with your credit card companies."

"I only have one."

"Really?"

"I like to keep things simple."

Rollins left the room.

I got up from the table and sat back down when a flood of hot pain gushed down my back and turned my vision dark and wavy. The nurse rushed over. Her lilac scent perked me right up. I wondered if I should try fainting and see how far she'd go to bring me back. She wasn't exactly Naomi Watts, but I've always had a special fondness for Lucy Liu and Michelle Yeoh.

"You should take it easy," she said softly. The smell of her minty mouthwash made me feel even better.

"Don't do anything stupid." Mr. Bedside Manner came over from the sink, wiping his hands with a white towel. "At least, not until the tests are in."

"I'll try my damnedest."

He left without another word.

The nurse put her face close. "I'll be back in a minute. Please. Stay here." She was gone before I could ask her if she'd mind giving me a backrub, sponge bath and shave.

By the looks of the day outside the small window, it was late morning. Which meant I'd been out of it all night. Which also meant I'd been whacked good.

All I could remember was that I'd been suckered in the men's room of Kelsey's. And, of course, the nice-looking chick hiding in the stall.

Why the hell was a *chick* hiding in a men's room?

Especially in a dump like Kelsey's?

The little bald guy on the bar stool had caused all this. Because of him, I got my head split open. But I was certain he wasn't the one who'd suckered me. Whoever had done that was tall. I was nailed with something hard. The barrel of a gun, most likely.

Was it because they didn't want me back there? Or because I was asking questions?

Some people didn't like questions. Some didn't like people who asked them. And there were others who didn't like people who went to bars and didn't order anything. But all this seemed slightly heavy-handed for someone guilty of just child-support-dodging.

Next year I'd be forty. I'd already discovered it much harder to bounce back after a fall. Like the good doc had said, my head was hard. I'd been hit before, but who knew how many more blows I could take before my skull finally cracked?

So what happens now? Do I give Sandra Brandon back her money and tell her I'm no longer interested? That I'm getting a little old to be suckered so easily? That I don't jump back up as quickly as I used to?

Out of the corner of my eye, I caught a figure standing in the open doorway.

It was the brunette from last night.

I jerked my head. Another flash of jagged hot pain shot up the back of my neck. I closed my eyes and waited for it to subside. When I opened them again, I realized the figure had disappeared.

I jumped down from the table. A tidal wave of hot agony gushed heavily through my limbs. I grunted through it, as any heroic trooper would, while trudging across the room. The dizziness stormed right back, settling on my shoulders like a suffocating blanket. I leaned against the doorway for balance and gritted my teeth.

Then peered out into the crowded hall.

No sign of the brunette.

Chapter 3

My Orange Avenue office sits directly in the center of a strip mall built in place of an old restaurant, an abandoned tire shop and two old homes bought by a developer about ten years ago.

Three other stores--a tee shirt shop operated by Hispanics, a liquor store owned by an elderly Jewish gentleman and his sons and a Chinese takeout restaurant run by a family of eight from Hong Kong--serve as my neighbors. The vacant store on the far end of the mall has been five different businesses during the last three years. For the last six months, the sign *THIS SPACE FOR RENT* has covered its front window.

Being patriotic, I frequently use the local facilities to keep the American dream alive and well. I visit the liquor store almost daily, buy moo goo gai pan and egg rolls three days a week and own several sweatshirts with my name printed in bold black letters on back. But I only wear them around the apartment.

Walking around in public wearing a shirt with your name on it seems tacky.

Whenever I swivel my chair around--and the parking lot isn't filled with the hungry lunch crowd wanting Chinese, of course--I have a clear view of the busy stretch separating the mall from the other businesses on the other side of the street.

Orange Avenue provides a rich source of daily entertainment. It's a one-way street, but on many occasions--usually around the lunch or dinner hours--you can be treated to a large dose of total brainlessness as a foreigner in a rental car attempts to brave traffic from the opposite direction. Sometimes the results are a little gory--a multi-vehicle pileup, with ambulance intervention. Other times, if OPD can get there before the foreigner is yanked from his vehicle by angry motorists, the story ends in a boring, predictable fashion.

But it's worthwhile entertainment during a meal of moo goo gai pan, egg rolls and a satisfying glass of Jack Daniel's.

The heavy traffic presently reached a standstill. A short, paunchy dark-haired guy around forty had abandoned his compact to take his opened map for a walk to the tire shop across the street. The map was a clear indication that the man was a tourist. Even without the map, the seasoned detective in me could easily tell something was amiss. It isn't wise to abandon your car in heavy traffic. It tends to irritate the other motorists. And as every Floridian knows, the average Florida driver is not the most patient in the world.

I had a sip of Jack's from the new bottle I'd just bought next door, courtesy of Sandra Brandon. It was a little early in the day for booze but I figured I deserved it. Having your head cracked open and then being dumped on the Courthouse steps entitles you to some quirkiness. Besides, a sip or two of Jack's always helps when things don't make sense. Sometimes it makes me think more clearly. Even if it doesn't, I find that after a while I no longer care.

And if I drink enough, I eventually realize that I no longer remember what's bothering me.

Outside, two visibly enraged motorists had gotten out of their cars to push the compact out of the way. A motorcycle cop appeared, parked along the curb and pulled his ticket book from his jacket pocket. He snatched his radio, said something to it, then opened his book.

The thumping in my head had eased up. The aspirins the Asian babe gave me were finally working. Maybe it was the Jack's. Or it could be my hard head triumphing after all.

But that didn't matter, either. I was too busy trying to figure out what happened the night before.

You really need to get out of here . . .

Hmmm . . . A clear indication that the woman knew what was about to happen.

But how?

Better yet, why was she there in the first place?

She definitely had the look of someone doing her best to become invisible.

She also looked familiar. I know I'd seen that face before. I couldn't remember where, but I'd seen it.

Whoever she was, she seemed tense. The eye-darting, the pale skin, the trembling--all dead giveaways. I remembered that look from grade school, when someone did something they didn't want the teacher to see. Or flunked a crucial test. That feeling of *oh, shit*! hung heavily in the air.

Besides, she was standing in a stall.

But the door was open.

If she was hiding, why was the door open?

A hooker waiting for a trick?

A definite possibility.

But in the *men's room*?

My superior instincts told me she wasn't a hooker. I guess I was just a hopeless optimist and wanted to see beauty and order in the world. But in my profession, you couldn't find much beauty or order. And in the places I visited, all I found were hookers, pimps, and drunks. The more money I was paid, the less beauty and order I found.

I didn't find *any* beauty or order at Kelsey's last night. Not in the bar or in the men's room. The brunette was beautiful in a lost, pitiful sort of way but was far from orderly.

And I surely didn't find beauty or order when I was hit over the head.

Unless, of course, I counted my dream with Naomi Watts.

The big question of all made no sense whatsoever. Who would care about someone asking questions about Don Brandon? Why risk pounding a guy senseless just because he wanted to ask a few questions about a deadbeat dad?

Unless Brandon was the one who did it.

He was a "bad boy." Pounding someone over a few questions would put him in good standing with the other "bad boys" in the area.

Who else would care that much?

More important, who would care that I was lying unconscious on the Courthouse steps?

No one in that area would worry about someone being hauled off and dumped. And since mostly everyone was probably drunk or working on it at that time of night, they probably didn't even know what they saw.

So how did I end up in the hospital?

The brunette? It only made sense. The gents who'd roughed me up were probably the same dudes who took my wallet and gun. I was surprised they hadn't taken my car keys. Good thing I knew how to hide them. Whenever I had to visit the wrong section of town, I always hid my keys in the small side pocket of my scuffed sneakers.

Good move, too. I'd freak if someone stole my classic TransAm.

Which reminded me--I had to take a cab to go back and fetch it before someone decided to have some fun using the windows for target practice.

The brunette probably reported the mugging. It might explain why she showed up in the hospital this morning.

But why would she leave so suddenly?

Was I imagining all this?

It was possible, wasn't it? I had helluva lump on my head. They said it was only a slight concussion, but they also said there might have been temporary damage to various parts of my brain. They weren't quite sure which parts would be affected and said it might take time before everything returned to normal. They also said I might not have even sustained *any* temporary damage. When I asked them why they were so

30

vague about everything, they gave me all sorts of complicated medical explanations.

I decided I imagined the brunette in the doorway.

Anything was possible when you were hit over the head, woke up in an emergency ward and were tended to by a tone-deaf doctor with the bedside manner of Gregory House.

All this thinking made my goose egg hurt again.

I needed something to eat. My favorite breakfast place sat right across the street, next to the tire place. They made great omelets, pancakes and coffee. A big breakfast might make me feel better. Then I could come back and make my call to Sandra Brandon. She should know that her good money wasn't being used to its fullest potential. The man she'd given a thousand bucks was getting a little long in the tooth for the rough stuff and would probably need a few days to recover from the golf ball-sized goose egg he was carrying around.

But first, I had to go back to Hughey and pick up my car. Then I'd drive right back and have breakfast.

I made the call to the cab service. Twenty minutes, they said. That's what they'd said at the hospital, too, before they'd shown up to haul my butt the two short miles to my office. Cab terminology is similar to towing service terminology. Twenty minutes almost always means an hour. But these guys were fairly good. When they said twenty minutes, it invariably meant forty-five.

With the help of the small pocket mirror I kept in my desk for emergencies, I straightened out my hair. I also adjusted my shirt collar and splashed some Stetson on my cheeks to cover up my whiskey breath.

I slipped a Count Basie CD into my portable on the corner shelf behind my desk and mellowed to some classic jazz while waiting for my cab.

***

Smilin' Susie's, a revamped Waffle House bought last year by a private investor, grinned proudly behind its fresh paint job.

Its outside walls were now a burnt orange, its shutters a golden-brown. It appeared much homier and inviting. The setup inside hadn't changed much, although it regularly did more business than its predecessor. It employed better waitresses, offered bigger portions of food and didn't make you wait long for service.

Smilin' Susie's served breakfast twenty-four hours a day. The long, narrow room smelled strongly of fried bacon and sausage even though it was nearly lunchtime.

I found a booth just inside the door.

Iris waddled right over and brought me coffee. When she spotted the bandage on the back of my head, her eyes bulged. "What happened, baby? Get in a fight?"

"I cut myself shaving."

"You're kidding, right?"

"I never could fool you, could I?"

She shook her head. "Sure looks painful."

"It doesn't feel too great, either."

"You gonna be okay?"

"I will be when I have something to eat."

"No problem. What can we get you?"

"How about two eggs over easy, whole-wheat toast, bacon and a couple of sausage patties? And lots of coffee."

"You betcha." She hurried off.

A moment later she placed a white carafe on the table and whisked off to get my order ready.

Their coffee was really strong. I gave it two sugars. It needed one more. Perfect. After a few more cups and a big breakfast, I'd be almost as good as new. The goose egg on my head would still be there, but the eternal optimist in me decided that if I didn't bother it, it might leave me alone as well.

A shadow near the front door caught my attention.

The brunette from Kelsey's men's room walked over and sat down at my table.

She looked a lot better in the sunlight. But it was really no wonder. How breathtaking can you be, hiding in a poorly lit bathroom stall? And anyway, I was supposed to be experiencing brain injury issues, so I figured everything I remembered from last night should be a *little* off.

Her dark-brown hair spilled over her shoulders, cascading down her back. Since she faced me, I couldn't tell exactly how long it was. Her big brown almond eyes held that same haunting quality I saw last night. She wore jeans and a black tank top. Her breasts were small but nicely shaped, her skin tanned and blemish-free. She wore the same golden necklaces as last night and carried a small black leather handbag, which she placed in her lap. She wore no rings.

I couldn't help staring.

"You're okay?" she asked.

"Just peachy. Except for this irritating lump sticking out of my head."

The middle-aged woman at the next table and her companion--another woman, a few years younger--watched me curiously. I wondered if I had stains on my shirt I hadn't noticed before.

"Does it hurt much?" the brunette asked.

"Only when I laugh." I figured a little levity would help the moment.

"I was worried."

"About what?"

"You."

"Why'd you leave the hospital?"

"I just wanted to . . . to make sure you were okay. I didn't want to complicate things."

"How?"

"I didn't want to answer any questions. Someone might think I knew about what happened."

"Like that cop Rollins?"

"Exactly."

"So you don't *know* what happened?"

"Just that someone was coming." She sighed. "I wish I could've done something to help."

"You did tell me to get out."

34

Another table of patrons watched me. I checked out my shirt but didn't find anything out of the ordinary.

So why was everyone staring?

"What's wrong?" she asked.

"Did I spill something on my shirt when I wasn't looking?"

"No. Why?"

I shrugged. "Maybe it's my stunning good looks."

"What?"

"Just being witty." I figured our neighbors were hungry for gossip so I decided to force them to find it somewhere else. I rested my elbows on the table, kept my hands in front of my face and lowered my voice. "I take it you closed the stall door right away."

She just looked at me.

"Otherwise, they would've seen you."

She nodded. She acted like she didn't know what I was talking about. Either that or she was lying and actually knew who'd busted in and cracked me over the head. Since that was something I didn't want to think about, I decided to get off the subject.

"Anyway, I'm glad they didn't see you. Who knows what they might've done if they'd found a female in there?"

"Like I said, I was worried. I was afraid they'd killed you."

"This brings me to the obvious question . . ."

She looked down at her lap. "You . . . want to know why I was there . . ."

"That's a really good guess."

"I . . . don't know how to tell you."

Iris came over. "You okay?"

"I'm fine, thanks. Why?"

Iris stared at the brunette, then at me again. "You sure?"

"What's the problem?" The middle-aged woman and the others still focused on me. "And why's everyone staring?"

Iris shook her head. "You *sure* you're okay, honey? You did get hit on the head, you know."

"I know. I was there, too. And even if I forgot, I'd say the bandage is a pretty damned good reminder, wouldn't you?"

Iris sighed.

It suddenly dawned on me that she hadn't brought a menu for the brunette. "Tell me something," I whispered.

Iris bent down and moved her face closer. "What is it?"

"Don't you want to know if the lady wants breakfast?"

Iris blinked. "What lady, baby?"

I started to point when I suddenly realized I was sitting by myself.

I did a quick scan of the room, the hall leading to the rest rooms and the front entrance. Then, on a whim, I checked underneath the table. I figured that if she could hide in a men's room, she could also hide underneath a table.

No sign of her.

"Where'd she go? And why'd she leave so soon?"

"Who, baby?" Iris stared anxiously at me.

"You're not kidding, are you?"

"About what?"

That was when I realized why everyone was staring.

I'd apparently been talking to someone who wasn't even there.

Chapter 4

When I got back to the office, my Audix was blinking with three messages.

One was from Sandra Brandon. One was from my friend, OPD Detective Neil Haversack. The last one was from my mother, who lived in a condo in Fort Lauderdale.

The message from Sandra Brandon, a simple "call me back," was her way of requesting status. Neil's "call my office when you get a chance" told me he wanted to know what happened last night. My mother's message--"just to let you know I'm still alive and would like to hear from you once in a while"--was identical to the other dozen or so she sent me each month.

I was still spooked over the incident with the vanishing brunette and didn't want to even try and focus on my mother, Neil or even Sandra Brandon. Instead of answering anyone--as any normal, conscientious man would do--I sat down, stared at the heavy traffic through the glass window and pondered the events of the last fifteen hours.

Was I going crazy? Or had the tap to my head rearranged a few vitally important message centers up there?

I didn't want to believe I might actually be hallucinating. I also didn't want to believe that my hallucination involved a hot-looking brunette. But what I didn't want to believe most of all was that

38

my hallucinations apparently had started *before* my tap on the head.

They'd started in the men's room with the brunette and resumed in the hospital after I woke up. Then, when I least expected it, they continued to flourish in my favorite restaurant, where I apparently carried on a pleasant conversation with myself in front of twenty people.

Maybe that tap *had* scrambled my brains. But if it had, it scrambled the part of my memory in charge of handling the sequence of events in order. It had upset them and made a total mess of my method of recall.

Weird, to say the least.

Scary, too. It made me wonder if I was going to mess up dates, appointments and phone calls.

Oh well. That's what voicemail was for.

The phone rang, thank God, before I had the chance to plunge into serious brain overload.

"Have you found my ex-husband yet?" Sandra Brandon asked in her usual sharp masculine tone.

"Not yet," I said pleasantly. "And a wonderful good afternoon to you as well."

"Whatever. Any progress?"

"Not so far." I decided not to ask if someone had pissed in her morning oatmeal when she wasn't looking. "But the day's young."

"I was hoping you might've heard something by now."

"I came across someone last night. I'm not sure it was your ex."

"You still have that photo I gave you?"

39

"Right next to my heart."

A pause. "Huh?"

"In my jacket pocket."

She sighed. My humor had taxed her again. "Well, if you still have it, why--"

"I didn't get a good clear picture."

"You weren't close enough?"

"Actually, I was close enough to hear the man's gut sounds."

"Then what stopped you from figuring out if it was Don?"

"I think it was the barrel of a gun. Or maybe a leather sap they used in those old detective shows."

Silence. Trying to digest that one, no doubt.

"What happened?"

"I was hit over the back of the head, dumped on the Courthouse steps and rushed to ORMC later on."

"Shit." She sounded more disgusted than concerned. "*Don* did that?"

"Like I said, I didn't actually see--"

"Are you all right?"

"That's a matter of opinion."

"Where are you now? The hospital?"

"In my office. I'll be all right."

Silence. She was probably deciding what to say next. My guess was that she didn't want to sound *too* coldhearted but didn't want any delays in finding her ex-husband. If she had any couth, she'd say she was really glad I was all right and that I should take off a few days and resume the case when I was feeling better.

"Well, what about my ex-husband?" she asked. "You don't need to take any time off, do you?"

At least she didn't let herself be distracted by overwhelming emotion. I was glad I hadn't upset her *too* much.

"Professional sleuths don't need time off," I explained patiently. "We just force ourselves to heal faster than normal people so we can continue wandering around in dangerous places, looking for dangerous types to sneak up on us."

Silence again. I'd either confused her or she'd switched the phone to the other ear.

"I've still got a lead or two. I'll track him down."

"How are you for money? The retainer I gave you . . . do you have any left?"

"I'll let you know if I need more."

"Whatever." She hung up.

I actually found myself feeling badly for her ex-husband. Many men pushed too far by a demanding woman often did things they wouldn't normally do. Which, in my opinion, explained the steady rise in the murder and assault rate during the last few years.

Don Brandon was a street punk, had kids with several other women and had obviously never been a sterling example of responsibility . . .

But in all fairness, he could quite possibly be one of those men pushed too far by the wrong female.

Sandra Brandon was not exactly the type of woman who brought out the best qualities in a man.

41

Chapter 5

At eight o'clock that night, Vesper's Vixens indulged in its usual chaotic madness.

The huge front lot glittered with shiny new Jaguars, Porsches, BMWs, Mercedes, and Corvettes, most of them leased by young software execs who thought nothing of spending hundreds of dollars each night on booze and lap dances.

I parked the TransAm about four rows down from the well-lit front entrance. I still felt weird about what was happening to my brain. I felt even weirder about what happened at Smilin' Susie's. I wanted to believe my hallucination was real. And why shouldn't I? That hallucination was better than any dream I'd ever had before. How many people can hallucinate a good-looking brunette that vividly?

But the skeptic in me told me she was much too good to be true.

That was a shame. Not only because she was pretty--or because she had a soft, sexy voice. Or even because she had the type of body I wanted to see naked. Those were certainly important factors, but what really nailed it for me was that she'd shown up in Smilin' Susie's, carried on a pretty damned realistic conversation with me, then disappeared like a puff of smoke.

I didn't need such complications in my life. I was a simple guy with simple tastes. Give me a simple case--a missing ex-wife or teenage daughter--and I was happy. Give me a little spending money and I'll follow you around anywhere. I'm the guy you go to when you want to find out if your wife is sleeping around. Or need to find someone and don't have the time to look him up yourself in Google, Reunion.com or the Social Security Registry. I was no hero. Looking down the barrel of a gun or being roughed up just didn't turn me on. Leave all the nasty stuff to the bigger, younger, more masochistic private eyes.

Finding a deadbeat bad boy like Brandon clearly defined the limits of my expertise. I'd already been roughed up because of it and wasn't happy for the experience. I didn't want to risk my life getting involved in anything more serious. Especially if it meant crossing the line and going somewhere I didn't belong. I carry a gun, but that didn't mean I was comfortable getting it out and actually *pointing* it at someone.

My cell beeped. The display said *MOM*.

Jeez . . . I wished she'd quit calling me when I was working. She knew what I did for a living. She also knew that I couldn't always call her whenever she wanted me to.

But I couldn't very well ignore her.

How can anyone ignore their mom?

I clicked it on. "Hi, Mom. Yes I'm eating well and no, I'm not messing around with those girls working on the Trail."

"How come you didn't return my call this morning?" She sounded as annoyed as usual. Which wasn't new to me at all. I'd been annoying my mother all my life.

43

But I had to choose my words wisely in this case. Telling your mother you were hit over the head and dumped was not the sort of thing that would get her off the line. If anything, it would get her on the first plane to Orlando. Having your mother disrupting your life during a case was not the best thing a private eye could do to earn his money. *Or* his reputation.

But I could never lie to her, so I decided to be vague. Vague usually worked with most mothers.

"I'm busy working a case."

"Too busy to give a couple of minutes of your time to the woman who suffered eight hours of labor to deliver you into this world?"

I sighed. That labor guilt-thing had gotten old long ago. "It's been a hectic day. Was there something you--"

"You're really eating well?" She sounded doubtful.

"Actually, as well as I can under the--"

"I'll bet you're still buying that fast food crapola."

"Pretty much. I really don't have the time to--"

"You *make* the time for your stomach, Ralphie."

I hated when she called me Ralphie. She'd been calling me that since I was five. She obviously still thought I was five. But how can you tell your mother you're not five any more without hurting her feelings? She *so* wanted me to *stay* five. Possibly for the rest of my life. "Yes, mom . . ."

44

"You should know about all that by now. Look at your poor father. Doughnuts and coffee for breakfast, coffee, and cigarettes all day long at the shop, then beer and whiskey after dinner every night. No wonder he dropped dead at fifty-three--"

"I know, Mom. I was there, remember?"

"I remember. I just think you forget things sometimes."

"I really don't." Her *when you coming to see me?* speech was about to hit me. I braced myself.

"So . . . when you coming to see me? It's been months now, and you haven't seen your mother or *any* of your relatives--"

"It's been *three weeks*--"

"It was in *April*, Ralphie. This is late *June*."

"Mom, I really can't talk right now."

"It's that stupid job, isn't it? That cowboy and Indian thing."

I sighed. "Cops and robbers."

"I *knew* I should've let you play more with those toys you wanted when you were little, but most of that stuff was so--"

"Dangerous. Yes, Mom. I know."

"It might have cured you of whatever you're going through now."

"What am I going through?"

"The same nonsense, only with grown-up nasty boys that should know better. Bad people that weren't raised right. They should be in prison. I still can't believe my baby boy--"

"I'm almost forty, Mom."

45

"--Is running around, chasing those nasty people--"

"Someone's got to do it."

"You be careful, Ralphie. You're all I have now, you know."

"You've got Aunt Rose, Aunt Charlotte, Uncle Al and Uncle Nicky living in the same complex."

"It's not like having your only son living with you."

"I really do have to go."

"I just made a fresh batch of *gnocchi's*. Just the way you like them. You know, with the extra garlic? You know they don't keep very well in the freezer. Not fresh, anyway."

Mom had been trying to bribe me with food since I was a kid. Why did I think she'd ever stop once I grew up?

"I'll be stopping by soon."

"When will you call again so we can have more time to talk?"

"Soon."

She gave me one of her deep sighs. "I guess that'll have to do."

"I mean it. I'll call you."

"And be careful. I know what that Orlando town is like. All my friends say the same thing. It's crawling with those drug people, vagrants and illegals. Everyone knows how crazy they are."

"Who? The drug people? The vagrants? Or the illegals?"

"*All* of them. And don't forget those tourists. They're even crazier than the illegals."

46

"I'll be careful."

"Call me."

"I will."

"And eat better. Take the time. *Enjoy* your food." She hung up.

I took the .380 Beretta Cheetah out of the console and checked the clip. Seven there, one up the pipe. Earlier I'd called OPD and gave them the serial number of the stolen Bersa. Lucky thing I had a few extra pistols handy. Hopefully I wouldn't need a gun for this.

Why should I need a gun to ask a few questions?

If I needed a gun, it meant Sandra Brandon's ex was definitely involved with some scary people. And I was definitely better off waiting for another less risky job to show up on my doorstep.

I considered the previous night a fluke. I'd probably pissed off the barman. Or maybe the bald-headed character perched on the barstool.

But I had to find out about this, one way or the other.

My pulse pounded as I slipped the Beretta inside my Uncle Mike's Sidekick holster beneath my left armpit. I zipped up my lightweight jacket in spite of the 78-degree mugginess and got out of the car.

***

Two huge muscleheads in ill-fitting dark suits blocked the double doors.

One resembled Arnold Schwarzenegger in the face and physique but gave the distinct impression he wasn't overburdened with brain cell activity. "Ten bucks, cover," he said in a bored voice.

I handed him a ten. "You weren't bad in *Terminator*."

"I get that a lot," he said flatly.

"So do I," his partner said.

I thought the second guy looked more like Billy Crystal on steroids, but I didn't want to be thrown out of the place before I could even get in.

"You two ought to be in movies." I hoped my empty compliment would urge them to give me back the ten and tell me to go in and enjoy myself on the house.

Instead, they both stared at one another as if evaluating each other for a movie role. Then gave me the same sort of evaluation, possibly to see if I was kidding. I thought the *Terminator*-looking guy would say something. He just pushed open the wide, stained wooden door.

Inside, the big place blinked and sizzled beneath a fireworks display of colored lights. Skinny, half-naked young women danced on the bar counter, in cages or on pedestals. Sweaty men in suits gripping wads of cash rushed toward an area marked *Lap Dancing*.

Sandra Brandon had said Don really liked this sort of high-brow entertainment.

I followed the anxious, panting crowd.

The semi-dark room pulsed with multicolored strobes rotating from a large metal apparatus mounted to the ceiling. A dozen men, their cheeks and foreheads moist with sweat, filled padded chairs

48

and fed cash to the naked dancers writhing sensuously above their laps.

I went over to the corner bar, where the disinterested barman tended to the few customers wanting to drink without the irritating distraction of a naked woman squatting over them. "You Lou?" I asked.

The barman didn't meet my eyes. "Who's asking?"

According to Sandra Brandon, Don did coke at Lou's West Orlando place while betting on backyard dog-fighting Lou's high-class neighbors had going each weekend. They might be buddies, but if they were anything like the other coke-snorting, dog-fighting aficionados I knew of, their friendship only went so far.

"My cool buddy Alexander," I said. I slid a ten across the counter.

The barman quickly pocketed the bill. That was a good start. "Your cool buddy got any brothers?"

"Depends."

"On what?"

"You got any cool answers for me?"

"Depends."

I groaned. This could go on indefinitely.

"On what?" I asked.

"On what the cool questions are."

"They'll be easy. Any first grader can answer them. I kinda think you might be safe."

The barman flinched. I'd probably twanged a nerve. "Lemme see a brother, first."

I slipped him another ten. "The first question--
"

"Not here." He jabbed a thumb toward the hall, where the restrooms were clearly marked. "We'll need privacy."

A blast of *déjà vu* exploded in my head. Rest rooms. Kelsey's.

My goose egg throbbed. If I didn't go back there with him, I'd be out twenty bucks and wouldn't have learned anything. I'd only brought fifty with me. If I was rolled again, I wouldn't be out much. But if I was hit in the same place and didn't die or turn into a walking veggie salad, I'd probably want to use the Beretta on this jerk and anyone else I came across on my way back out.

But I had to find out *some*thing. I figured that since I was already on my guard, it would be impossible for anyone to jump me this time.

It *sounded* reasonable, didn't it?

My pulse hastened as I followed the barman down the dimly lit hall. We went past the rest rooms on the right. Two payphones hung from the wall on the left. A door marked *OFFICE* formed a dead end.

More *déjà vu*.

Lou opened the door. The room was dark.

"You coming in or what?"

"It's *dark* in there."

"So?"

"I'm afraid of the dark."

"You're *what*?"

50

"It's something from my childhood days." I had no intention of going into a dark room with this boy or anyone else working here. "Too many scary movies at the local theater. You know how it is."

"Don't be an asshole. I don't have all night."

"I'll try not to be, but I'm still afraid of the dark."

He reached in and flicked on a light. The room blazed with light. "Better?"

"Much." I followed him through the doorway. My professional eyes took in everything quickly. A large mahogany desk, its blotter covered with ledgers. An expensive black leather adjustable chair. Filing cabinets. A polished cherry credenza--

The door slammed shut behind me.

A musty-smelling pillowcase was pushed roughly over my head. Whoever did it brushed my goose egg, which started up a pounding that jolted down my neck in a series of sharp electric zaps.

Gritting my teeth, I tried lashing out, but the goon behind me easily pinned my arms to my sides. I barely had time to be scared--or even evaluate the situation--when something large and solid slammed into my midsection, sending a hot wave of vibrating pain shimmering up and down my body.

A voice close to my face whispered, "This is how we treat dickheads who ask stupid questions."

I wanted to tell him I hadn't had the time to ask any but it's hard to say anything with the wind knocked out of you.

Someone rapped on the door.

The goon gripping my arms froze. "What *now*?" he whispered, his grip loosening slightly.

A muffled voice from outside said, "Lou? You in there?"

The voice in front of me muttered, "*Fuck* . . ."

The goon behind me: "We gotta *do* something--"

"I *know* it, moron . . ."

The muffled voice said, "Phone call."

I wanted to tell them that I'd wait here until they were finished with their phone call but I was still trying to get my breath back.

The goon behind me let go of my arms and pushed me to the floor. I heard the shuffling of feet. A door opened, then closed.

I pulled off the pillowcase.

I was alone in the room.

Darkness. They'd turned off the light.

My throbbing gut fussed at me. I crawled over to the door and pressed my ear against it. The slamming of another door echoed down the hall. Then silence.

I reached up and cracked open the door.

The dimly lit hall was empty.

Chapter 6

My senses in serious overload, I went back out to the lap dancing area.

If I'd been smart, I would've used the other hall, gone back to the main room and hightailed it to the parking lot.

But I decided to finish what I'd been paid to do.

Or maybe I was a glutton for punishment. Whatever it was, I wanted to ask Lou why he'd felt the need for theatrics when I just wanted to ask him a few questions about his friend Don. He had no idea what I had in mind. Just because I knew they did coke and enjoyed good-natured dog-fighting didn't mean I was going to ask about it or cause trouble. Since I was a dog lover, I wanted to cause a *bunch* of trouble. I might even find out the details later on and get together with OPD to organize a raid. And since these goons had just altered the game plan, I might just do that.

But that had nothing to do with now. I was being paid to perform a specific task and intended to stick to it. The task required me to ask a few questions. I wanted to ask if Lou had seen Don lately or knew where he was living now. I might have wanted to tell him about a babe who'd asked me to set her up with him, for all he knew. The fact that I was willing to pay for a little information didn't mean I wanted Lou's ass as well. All that pillowcase nonsense told me was that if Lou was prepared to rough me up for very little reason, he'd done something he didn't want anyone to know about.

It pays to find out a little about someone before you rough him up.

But no matter what his reasoning was, he'd forced my hand. I'd just given him twenty bucks and all I got out of it was a brief trip to the office and a sucker punch to the gut. I figured he owed me one or two good answers.

The room still rocked. An endless supply of horny men waited in line to toss money at good-looking naked women they couldn't even have sex with.

Whoever said men were stupid certainly knew what they were talking about.

Lou was gone--replaced by another large, stupid-looking barman. I wondered if these places specifically employed men who were large and stupid-looking.

Lou's replacement had no idea where Lou had gone. I didn't bother slipping him a ten--I had no intention of paying anyone else to rough me up.

It was late, so I had no choice but call it a night.

Part of me was glad. I was tired and still sore from the sucker punch, and my joints ached from being manhandled and pushed to the office floor. I didn't want to even consider doing this again for a while.

What puzzled me most about the whole business was the man who'd knocked on the door during the scuffle.

I couldn't help thinking of the Cavalry showing up at a crucial moment in a Western. I realized this was my imagination working overtime, so I tried dismissing it. Coincidence. Nothing but. Vesper's was a busy place. People phoned people all the time. I just happened to be lucky enough to be in the right place and the right situation at that particular moment.

By the time I got back to my South Conway apartment, it was nearly midnight. I was beat, my head hurt and my ribs still ached.

Worst of all, my thoughts kept looping.

Despite the scuffle, the swelling on the back of my head had gone down. I gently touched the bandage covering it. Still tender, but tolerable. I dry-swallowed three aspirin from the bottle in the medicine cabinet just for good measure and went back into the bedroom.

Miles Davis's *Sketches of Spain* seemed just right for my present mood. I was a jazz buff; listening to my favorite guys helped me relax. Miles was good for that. Brubeck was even better, but all my Brubeck's were in the living room and I was too lazy to make the long trip down the hall to look for them.

"Will O' the Wisp" started up. I turned down the volume to just barely audible and sat down on the bed to take off my shoes and socks. Tomorrow I'd return to Vesper's. Maybe Lou would be in a more receptive mood. One thing I'd learned about this business--persistence got you results. Either you got answers or found yourself dead or lying unconscious on the Courthouse steps. But if you weren't persistent, you got nothing.

The phone rang.

The clock on the nightstand said it was past one a.m. Who'd be calling at this hour? I checked the display. *Unknown name, unknown number.*

I picked up. "This better be good."

A woman's voice: "Are you all right?"

The brunette?

Impossible. How could a hallucination use a phone?

"Who *is* this?"

"I think you know."

"If I did, I wouldn't have asked."

A pause. "I'm glad you're all right."

"Why wouldn't I be?"

Silence.

"Is there some reason why you keep popping up out of the blue and making me think you're real when you actually aren't?"

Another pause. "What makes you think I'm not?"

"That vanishing act you pulled at Smilin' Susie's this morning, for one thing."

"I was there, wasn't I?"

"Until I looked away. That Houdini you maneuvered brought tears to my eyes and goose pimples to my flesh. How'd you do it? I didn't see any mirrors."

"I . . . had to leave."

"Without a good-bye, so long or Abyssinia?"

"I had to leave quickly."

"Without a good-bye, so long or Abyssinia?"

Silence.

"Are you ignoring me? Or trying to think up a really nifty answer?"

"I'm just grateful you're okay. You could've been hurt tonight. Vesper's is a rough place. Those people . . . they're *mean*."

How the hell did she know I was at Vesper's?

"How'd you know where I was?"

"I . . . just knew . . ."

"Did you call them tonight and ask for Lou?"

A pause. "You really need to stay away from places like that."

"You're not answering my questions."

She sighed. "Please tell me you'll be more careful . . ."

I felt like I was talking to my mother again. This girl was just as cooperative as Mom was. "Listen . . . I'm a detective. I'm *paid* to go to bad places and do people's dirty work for them. I can't do half the things I'm being paid to do if I'm careful. I don't like a lot of the stuff I have to do but it pays the bills. I don't go out of my way looking for ways to get beaten up or slapped around, but there are circumstances when I have to deal with people I shouldn't turn my back on."

"Well, you obviously turned your back on the wrong person tonight."

Damn. "How do you *know* all this stuff?"

"Please be more careful, all right?"

"Only if you tell me who you are. And while you're at it, you might as well tell me why you care

57

so much. If you're just a hallucination, you wouldn't care at all."

She hung up.

This was getting really old.

Chapter 7

After a restless night, I got up just before ten.

Finding the bathroom in a one-bedroom, one-bath apartment doesn't normally require much investigation--especially for a dynamite private eye. And since I've been living in the same place for two years, I can usually find the john blindfolded, or even falling-down drunk. A few steps out into the hall, then another step through the bathroom doorway, always gets the job done.

But this morning, I stood in the middle of the hall, totally naked, wondering what I was doing. My hallucination's phone call the night before had freaked me totally. I couldn't help wondering how she knew so much about me. How she knew where I'd gone, what I'd done. That I'd been suckered.

That sudden phone call at Vesper's baffled me. Even though my hallucination hadn't been very clear about what happened, I knew damned well she was the one who'd called. But I had no idea *why* she'd called or why she'd called at that particular moment. I just knew deep-down that it was her.

She also knew when I'd gotten home. Since she was just a hallucination and since a sane man usually doesn't hand out his business card to a hallucination, how did she find my number? How did she know where I live?

More importantly, how did she know when I got home?

Did the fact that it was one in the morning have anything to do with this?

Maybe she just guessed that I'd be home by one. Since she obviously knew I was at Vesper's and also knew where I lived, a quick calculation would tell her roughly how long it would take me to get home.

Pretty calculated reasoning--especially for someone who wasn't there in the first place.

But if she wasn't *really* there, maybe I just *imagined* the phone call.

But what about the conversation?

That didn't prove anything. Conversation had already taken place earlier, at Smilin' Susie's. If I could imagine a conversation in a crowded restaurant, I sure as hell could imagine one in my own apartment.

After an agonizing five minutes huddled beneath the warm shower spray--which proved tricky, since I had to keep my bandage dry--I toweled off and dressed.

While the coffee brewed, I picked up the phone and dialed the extension for my friend Neil Haversack at OPD.

"What're *you* up to these days?" asked the soft, low-pitched voice.

"Besides being beat up, robbed and dumped? Not much."

"I heard. Why didn't you return my call yesterday?"

"I was much too busy."

"Doing what?"

"Getting beat up again."

"Aren't you getting a little old for that sort of thing?"

"Subtle, my friend. Very subtle."

"Hey, you're forty."

"Bite your tongue."

"Couple of months, right?"

I sighed. "Forty isn't old."

"It is when you're up against guys fifteen years younger, six inches taller and fifty pounds heavier."

"Your point?"

"You're up against guys fifteen years younger--
"

"Everyone needs *some* sort of hobby."

"What's wrong with jogging? Or tennis? Stamp-collecting's just the thing if you want to protect the old bones. I even know some guys your age who like riding the mechanical bull in some of these low-class dives."

"Not enough excitement."

"*Please* . . ."

"I *like* making occasional trips to the hospital. Sometimes they even let me turn on the siren."

"One or two more of those *occasional trips* and you won't have the brains left to figure out what you're doing."

"I'll try to remember that."

"Clever. But listen . . . there are some dangerous characters in this town who'd kill their own mother for pocket change."

"There are dangerous characters everywhere."

"Maybe, but people seem to be getting nuttier."

"It's the heat. The humidity. The hurricanes. The high taxes."

"Personally, I think it's the drugs coming in. Ninety percent of the cases we handle nowadays are drug-related."

"Just ninety?"

"That was a conservative guess. Off the record I'd put it closer to ninety-eight point five."

"Supply and demand."

"Unfortunately."

I wanted to tell Neil about my hallucination but knew it would be a mistake. He'd think my hospital trip had already scrambled what brains I had left. Besides, cops didn't believe in hallucinations.

"You gonna tell me what happened?" he asked.

"Didn't Rollins tell you?"

"Rollins said you were mugged. Not much else."

"A man of few words. I like that."

"That what happened?"

"Basically."

"Tell me what Rollins *didn't* tell me."

"I'm tracking a deadbeat dad. He hangs out at Vesper's, Kelsey's--all the best spots in town."

"You know who owns Vesper's, right?"

Everyone knew the local mob bought the place for an investment. It had been operating the last several years without much negative publicity. Most locals thought it was built for tax purposes and run by mob-financed managers and accountants in an effort to grab tourist money closer to town.

"Doesn't everyone?" I said.

"Just a little reminder to wrap your brain around while you're having all that fun on your ambulance trips."

"I'll keep it in a safe place. Away from the goose egg so it won't leak out."

"You okay now? Aside from the cracked skull?"

"A dynamite doctor shoved my brains back in and sewed my head shut before anything could leak back out."

"Glad to hear it. Sounds like you might be in a little over your head."

"When have you ever known me to be in over my head?"

"Ever since I've known you."

"How long's that been?"

"Can't remember. My memory's a little hazy lately."

"Off your feed? The doughnut shop closed this morning?"

"If I were you, I'd keep the smartass level down just a tad. My humor only stretches so far."

"Can't help it. I just had my brains rearranged and can't seem to find the boxes where I keep all my information about diplomacy."

"I didn't know you ever *had* any of that."

"I keep it in a safe place."

"Hidden real well, obviously."

"Don't want it getting into the wrong hands."

"Deacon, you've been running your mouth since I've known you. You can't suddenly blame it on a tap to the noggin at this stage."

"I've got to blame it on *some*thing."

"Just so long as you don't blame your mother. Don't forget, I've met the lady."

"She asks about you once in a while."

"Seen her lately?"

"Couple of months ago."

"Bet she loves that."

"She just called yesterday to remind me how much she does."

"Tell her I said hi when she calls again today or tomorrow."

"What makes you think--"

"Like I said, I've met the lady."

I fixed some scrambled eggs and rye toast and had more coffee. As soon as I finished doing the dishes, I called Sandra Brandon.

"Who's *this*?" Her raspy voice suggested she also had a bad night. But I couldn't imagine anyone sticking a pillowcase over her head and living to tell about it. "And why are you calling so damn early?"

"It's almost noon. I'm your favorite private eye. I'm calling because I'm up. Otherwise, I'd still be asleep, and this call would be nothing more than an insignificant blip in the stratosphere."

A sigh. She obviously couldn't appreciate my humor any better at home than in my office. "What do you want? Find that asshole yet?"

"Not yet."

"Then what do you want?"

I loved women who got to the point.

"I tried talking to Lou last night but he didn't want to be bothered."

"What'd he do?"

"Lured me to one of the back offices and tried beating the crap out of me."

"Sounds like something he'd do. He's just as bad as Don, you know. What did you ask him?"

"I didn't get a chance to ask him anything."

"You really need to stay away from him."

"That's what I was thinking. I didn't really think too seriously about it, though, until he stuck a pillowcase over my head."

"What the hell did he do *that* for?"

"It made it easier for him to punch me in the gut."

"You know, if you keep getting beat up, you'll *never* find Don."

"That makes really good sense." I was *so* glad she had everything figured out.

"Can't you just ask around without getting beat up?"

"You know something? That's a really terrific idea. I wish I'd thought of it."

"Is that why you called? To tell me you got beat up again?"

"I figured I'd call and let you know how the case is going."

"But you haven't found him yet."

"Not yet. But since you're a paying customer, I thought I should let you know about the progress I'm making."

"What progress? You keep getting beat up."

"You're absolutely right."

"Do me a favor."

"What's that?"

"Try and find him without getting beat up again, okay?"

She hung up.

I drank my third cup of coffee and stared at the phone. Hopefully, my hallucination wouldn't call again. I decided not to answer if it registered *Unknown Name, Unknown Number* again. I had things to do and didn't want another call from some strange woman who wasn't really there. It tended to disrupt my concentration. Bad enough trying to concentrate when you faced getting beaten up each time you slipped money to someone. It kind of put a slightly sinister slant to the term "American Dream."

I had to drive back to Vesper's if I wanted to find out anything. I didn't know if Lou would be there this early. Vesper's opened at noon and stayed open until two or three in the morning. The place ran at least two shifts. I was bound to learn *some*thing if I asked enough questions and irritated enough people.

As I said before, persistence is the name of the game.

Chapter 8

I pulled into the front lot and parked in a vacant space two rows down from the huge pink building.

Instead of going inside, I sat in the TransAm and tried slipping my mind into the professional state it needed to be in for sleuthing.

Focus on the job. Sandra Brandon, remember? Her deadbeat husband? A thousand bucks? Forget the phone call. Forget the brunette. How can you take a hallucination seriously in the first place? You were hit pretty hard. Remember that the next time you think you see her.

Concentrate on going inside and finding out about Brandon. And above all, watch your ass. You're a detective--start acting like one.

But no matter how hard I tried, I just couldn't stop wondering about the brunette. As much as I wanted to believe she was just a hallucination, I also hoped she wasn't. I didn't want to believe she was because, in doing so, I'd have to admit something was wrong with me. Maybe the blow to my head had indeed scrambled my brains. In that case, I could not only hang up my professional sleuthing, I'd have to hang up many other things, such as living alone, owning guns, getting drunk, driving wherever I wanted whenever I wanted, meeting women in bars and clubs--everything the average divorced guy in reasonably good health takes for granted. I couldn't tolerate living a supervised existence on a daily diet of meds and baby food. If

I had to live with my mother again, she'd successfully turn me back into an overgrown five-year-old in minutes.

But if the brunette *wasn't* a hallucination, who *was* she? How could she pop up and disappear so easily? Why didn't Iris see her? Why were the customers at Smilin' Susie's staring at me?

And if she *was* merely a delusion, why'd she call for an ambulance? Or show up at the hospital? Why would a delusion bother to find out where I was so she could call at the right moment to get Lou and his simian buddy off me? How could she manage a phone in the first place? How could she press the buttons? How could she hold the piece to an ear--or a mouth--that didn't exist?

This was way over the edge. I *had* to believe she wasn't real. I *had* to believe it because it was true. She *wasn't* real. No one else saw her. It was my imagination and the result of the concussion I'd suffered. And the fact that I thought I'd seen her before merely nailed it. She was probably the image of someone from my past emerging from the fog that filled my brain since my mishap in Kelsey's bathroom.

But whatever was happening to me, I had to suck it up and focus on what I was doing. A hallucination didn't change anything. I still had to find Brandon. It had started out as a job but had quickly become personal. If someone was trying to steer me off the case, there was a good reason for it.

Maybe Neil was right. Maybe I *was* getting in over my head.

But I just didn't feel like backing down now.

My dash clock said 12:21. The huge muscleheads bravely manned the double doors out front. Even at this distance I could tell they weren't the same sophisticated gents as the night before.

Someone approached my car.

"Hi," my hallucination said.

She wore cutoffs and one of those loose-fitting tops with a V-neck and no sleeves, showing off her small waist. The sort of picture that would cause most men to kill themselves on the road or go totally blank if they were just walking around. Her hair hung loose, falling over her shoulders and sliding down her arms with the warm breeze.

Yep, definitely the sort of body I wanted to see naked. Hallucination or not, she could easily cause me to do something really stupid without even trying.

Focus. She's not there. She's merely the result of that tap to your head. Remember that.

I forced myself to turn away. *The job, remember? Go in there and find someone who won't lure you back to the--*

"Not speaking to me today?" she asked.

Find Lou. If you can't find him, find someone who--

"I can't blame you." She sighed and looked all pouty. "I probably wouldn't want to bother with someone like me, either."

I hated when a woman went all pouty on me. My heart always stepped in and made me do stupid things. Females knew this trick since puberty--

which was why they were experts at it by the time they tried on their first training bra.

I figured a female hallucination was no different.

"You're only in my head," I muttered, mostly for my own benefit. I went right back to thinking about my next move.

"Like I said, I can't blame you."

"What am I supposed to think? I'm sitting there in a restaurant, talking to you. Then all of a sudden…"

"I told you. I had to leave."

"Without a word? Or proof that you were even there?"

"I thought it best if I just faded away."

"You really do that well, girl."

"I've had lots of practice."

"Good. Now that we've gotten everything straightened out and understand one another--"

"You *really* understand?" She sounded doubtful.

"I'm trying to convince myself that I do."

She nodded.

"Got it now?"

"I think so."

"Good. Now do your thing and fade."

"Before I go?"

"I'm listening."

"Lou's not there today."

"*What*?"

"His friends are."

"How could you possibly--"

70

"Those two standing out front."

How the hell did she *know*?

"Listen. If you're gonna keep warning me about--"

"The one on the left? He's the one you need to watch. The one on the right will ask for your money. The other will rabbit-punch you while your hand's in your pocket. If you're going in, I suggest you wait until another line forms outside. Make sure you're not the last in line. If you can make it inside, you'll be okay, but you don't know what'll happen once--"

"But how do you *know* all this?

"Lou told them about you. They know what you look like."

The two muscleheads were talking about something. No customers yet. If my hallucination was right, I'd better wait until a couple of cars showed up.

"Listen," I said. "It's not that I don't believe you--"

She'd disappeared.

Chapter 9

Felicia Hartland, president and CEO of Philo-Media Consultation Services, Inc., was known as Felicia Hartland-Deacon before our divorce just two short years ago.

During our marriage, Phil--which she's been called since grade school--kept busy juggling her time between monotonous housewife duties and brain-scorching college studies. I never quite figured out how she did it without becoming a babbling idiot, but she managed quite efficiently in our fifteen years together. The ten-year marriage might have lasted to this day, but when it finally dawned on her that I wasn't about to give up my sleuthing for a safer, more predictable nine-to-five office job, she decided our future together was doomed. My sporadic hours didn't help matters. Nor did the number of times I came home with a split lip or black eye.

She continued her education and earned a Master's in Business Management three years ago. She'd been running Philo-Media from the third floor of the National Bank Building in downtown Orlando ever since. Judging by the stock reports I caught periodically on the Dow, the fancy hand-painted signs decorating the doors on her floor and the huge potted plants adorning the wall near the elevators, she was doing extremely well. I hated admitting that, but it was true. I also hated admitting that her career took off like a scalded cat once our divorce was finalized.

Women have countless ways of destroying a man's ego.

Phil was dark-haired, velvet-skinned, slender, tiny-breasted and five-feet-ten. I'd never been partial to huge, smothering breasts, so her slender compactness was a turn-on for me. Her height was the only physical thing that caused problems during our marriage, since we were basically the same height. When she wanted to appear in public wearing six-inch spikes--which she did often--it fueled many an argument. It had nothing to do with any hint of inferiority on my end. I just thought that her being seen with a man who wasn't sufficiently taller than she was might cause her unnecessary embarrassment. I wasn't afraid of voicing my opinion on the matter.

She sat at her desk in a tailored brown suit and frilly cream blouse, smoking one of the sixty or so cigarettes she burned up in a normal day. Her hair was pulled back and fastened at the crown with a golden barrette. Several spiral tendrils had pulled loose and dangled free, bumping her sharp cheekbones each time she moved her head.

I sat down facing her desk. Framed photos covered its shiny surface. At least eight flanked each side of her laptop. I couldn't see who they were from my vantage point but had the feeling some were of me in my heyday and others of us in happier times. I didn't want to appear anxious, so I decided not to embarrass her by sneaking a peek.

Doing so might convey the message that I needed an ego boost. Due to the last couple of days, I did need an ego boost, but I didn't want her to know. At least, not yet.

Besides, both of us knew how photogenic I was, so there was really no need to appear unduly narcissistic.

"Weren't you smoking one of those the last time I saw you?" I asked.

"That's highly probable. Why?"

"Just an observation. It's what a detective does."

"I'm painfully aware of what a detective does. Or have you already forgotten the main reason I walked out of an otherwise wonderful marriage?"

I knew right then that I should've opened the conversation with something slightly chattier.

"Is that why you've come to see me? To remind me that I smoke? Or that you're obviously still a detective?"

I didn't reply; I was too busy trying to think up a clever line.

"You know about that modern invention they brought into production a few years back, don't you? The telephone? You could've saved yourself the price of a gallon of gas by using one."

"Funny how the human mind works, isn't it?"

"Hilarious. But something tells me you're here for some other reason."

"Such as?"

"Maybe you've finally come seeking my advice on why I think you should try another career."

74

"Why would I need that sort of advice?"

"Because you're here."

"Maybe I came to see how you're doing."

"You also look like you haven't been sleeping lately."

"Maybe I came here after an extremely rough morning to see how you're doing."

"You've also got a rather large bandage on the back of your head. I thought you hated fighting."

"I've changed my attitude about life and its many mysteries since we split up."

"Why is that?"

"Our divorce traumatized me."

"I'm sorry."

I shrugged. "A man's got to find *some* way of coping."

She pursed her lips as she always did when she suspected I might be holding back. Then she sucked on her cancer stick and blew a smoke ring in my direction. "I'm glad you've found a new hobby. Tired of playing your harmonica?"

I nudged the smoke ring away with my left hand. It broke into a wavy U before it was zapped by the overhead air-conditioning duct. "Why would I ever get tired of that?"

"You might have to if your new interest in physical violence destroys your embouchure."

"No need to worry."

"In *your* line of work?"

"I'm careful."

"I can see that. How many stitches this time?"

"As you can probably guess by its location, it won't affect my embouchure."

"This time, maybe."

"You can be *so* cynical . . ."

"When the occasion calls for it. And speaking of occasions . . ."

"You mean this one?"

"You always were perceptive."

"I have my moments."

"So you've decided to come here and *share* one of them?"

"Like I said, maybe I just wanted to see how you were doing."

"I highly doubt that."

"Why?"

She shrugged. "The fact that you're doing everything to avoid answering my question. I know you, Ralph. When something's really bothering you, you disguise everything with jokes and clever by-play."

"You'd make a good sleuth yourself."

She frowned. "Too many negatives."

"Like what? The erratic hours? The armed, doped-up bad guys? The sporadic pay? The insurance agents who won't return my calls?"

"That more or less sums it up."

"Every job has its negatives."

"Maybe not *every* job . . ."

"Name one."

She waved an arm. "Look at this office."

I reluctantly scanned the posh mauve carpet, the expensive prints, the designer furniture and the panoramic view of the skyscrapers embellishing the Orlando Beautiful skyline behind the polished cedar credenza. Everything was impressive, but Phil had to realize that there were more important things in life than success, achievement, money and a panoramic view.

"Your point?" I asked.

"I have my own hours, faithful employees, great camaraderie with clients, good pay and my own condo. Oh, I'm also able to buy a new car every other year."

"A miserable existence, at best."

"Still have that thirty-year-old TransAm?"

"It's a classic."

"It's *thirty*."

"You make thirty sound dirty."

"Thirty *is* dirty for a car. Unless it's a Vette or a T-Bird. Or maybe a Shelby."

"It's my most valuable possession."

"You want to tell me this time?" she said suddenly.

"Tell you what?"

"Why you came to see me."

I squirmed in the chair. The damned thing was one of those ergonomically correct thingamabobs that feels like a torture device if you try and get comfortable. I tilted my right hip and leaned back. There I was, doing a form of mild contortion in a thousand-dollar chair. "No *specific* reason--just that I think I'm going crazy."

"I've been telling you that for years."

"This time, I'm serious."

She picked up her ebony cigarette holder and screwed her half-smoked cancer stick into it. When she was busy talking, she sometimes forgot the holder. When she used it, she made the act of smoking an art form--like those old glossy ads they used in high-fashion magazines before Bobby Kennedy made smoking ads illegal. When Phil sat there, dressed to kill, her back arched, one long leg crossed over the other, she exuded the epitome of sophistication, and it didn't matter that she reeked of cigarette smoke. She watched me as she puffed away, searching my eyes, my facial expressions. Phil minored in Psychology.

"When did this sudden odyssey into oblivion happen?" she asked.

"No idea."

"I'm sure you could figure it out if you tried."

Easy for *her* to say. "I don't know where to begin."

"Try remembering the first thing that doesn't make sense, then work from there."

Sometimes she was no help whatsoever. "That'll take me back to when you said we needed to spend some time apart."

"When was that?"

"A week or so after you moved out of our apartment and a few days before I was served with the divorce papers."

"I'm sure what you're worrying about right now happened sometime after that."

"Some weird things happened long before that, too--now that we're on the subject."

78

"Such as?"

"Puberty was sort of a crazy time for me."

She sighed.

"Childhood was very traumatic as well."

She pushed out a thick billow of smoke and sat forward. "I have an appointment in half an hour. Think you can get to the point? Or should I just call them and cancel?"

It was time to just come right out with it. Phil was a bright woman. She might not even think I was going crazy. But if I *was* going crazy, I needed to find out quickly. But I couldn't find out unless I told someone. I didn't want to see a psychiatrist-- not yet, anyway. But I had to tell *some*one. Phil had always been a good listener. She might even be able to help.

And I did need help. This hallucination thing was affecting my performance. I shouldn't even be here. I should be at Vesper's, asking my questions and earning the money Sandra Brandon had given me. But when my hallucination showed up, I was so distracted that I couldn't even figure out what I was doing out there in the first place.

"I'm seeing hallucinations," I finally said.

Instead of dropping her jaw or blinking--as any normal, *caring* ex-wife would do-- she just sat there, giving me that look women give men when they want the guy to feel stupid.

"No comments?" I asked.

"I'm still listening."

"The least you could do is ask for details."

"I just assumed you were going to jump right in and provide them."

"I was. But you're just sitting there, giving me that look."

"Which look?"

"The one that makes me feel like some sort of oddity."

"What would you *like* me to do?"

"Ask me for details."

"All right." She cleared her throat--which made me feel even *more* like a clown. "What *sort* of hallucinations?"

"It's in the form of a mysterious brunette."

She nodded.

"What's *that* supposed to mean?"

"What's *what* supposed to mean?"

"That nod."

She shrugged. "It was just a nod."

"It didn't mean anything?"

"All it meant was, oh. Or, I see. Or, ah."

"You're sure?"

"C'mon, Ralph. What can you possibly read into a simple nod?"

"With most people? Not much. With you? A lot."

"Like what?"

"There's definitely a gi-normous I-told-you-so crawling around, waiting to be unleashed."

"Now why would I--"

"You've wanted to give me one of those for years."

"But why would I want to give you one right now? Especially when you're obviously so upset that you've come to me for help?"

"I don't know. I just get that feeling."

"That would make me callous and shallow, wouldn't it?"

I just sighed. Sometimes the woman was so bright, she scared me.

"But you know I'm *not* callous and shallow, don't you? We lived together nearly fifteen years. And if I really *was* callous and shallow, you wouldn't have come here. If you really *do* consider me callous and shallow and have come to me for help anyway, it wouldn't make you very bright, would it?"

"Damn, you're good."

She nodded again, but this time I didn't take issue with it.

"Now tell me about this hallucination. Where did you start seeing it?"

"In the men's room at Kelsey's Bar on Hughey."

She rested her elbows on the blotter. She wore several gold bracelets on each wrist and three rocks on each hand. Phil didn't come from money but knew where to look for it and, more important, where to find it. "You first saw this woman in a *men's* room?"

"How'd you know she's a woman? I didn't specify which sex she was, did I?"

"You wouldn't refer to a man with brown hair as a brunette. You would've said you were having

81

the hallucination of a brown-haired man you met in a men's room at Kelsey's. By the way, what were you doing *there*? That place is . . . *nasty*."

"Really? Thanks." It was refreshing, knowing so many people who could steer you away from the bad places in town.

"Why did you imagine a woman in the men's room?"

"I have no idea."

"What was she doing when you first saw her?"

"Doing?"

"She wasn't sitting down, was she? Using the facilities?"

"Don't be ridiculous."

"*I'm* not the one with the hallucination."

"She was standing in a stall."

"Just *standing* there?"

"That's right."

"Did she say anything?"

"She told me someone was about to come in, looking for me."

"Did that happen?"

I pointed to my bandage.

"She was right, then."

"Of course she was right."

"You should have listened to her."

"I was too busy being shocked."

"About what?"

"About stumbling upon a good-looking woman in a men's room--what else?"

"She was good-looking?"

82

"Of course she was good-looking. You can't expect me to dream up an *ugly* hallucination, can you?"

"Tell me more about her."

"I think I've seen her before."

"Before what?"

"Before the men's room thing."

"Where?"

"I wish I knew."

"Then how do you know--"

"I don't *know*, dammit." The frustration had flooded back. I wanted to jump up, pick up something and toss it through the window. But I knew I couldn't. It would definitely end our conversation. Phil hated violence. Occasionally a little hair-pulling or ass-swatting between the sheets, but nothing more strenuous. "I just know I've seen her before."

"Why so defensive, Ralph? I wasn't there, remember?"

"Sorry. This has been traumatic."

"Of course it has."

"Other things have happened, too."

"Such as?"

"She's been popping up ever since."

"Popping *up*?"

"Like *I Dream of Jeannie*."

"And you've come to ask me what to do about this?"

"What's wrong with that?"

"Ralph, I'm your ex-wife--not a licensed psychiatrist."

"You studied Psychology."

"I'm not licensed."

"You think I need--"

"I don't know. Do *you*?"

"Sometimes you *sound* like a licensed psychiatrist."

"What did the ER doctors say about your head injury? This might have something to do with that, you know."

"I don't *think* so . . ."

"Why not?"

"I saw her *before* I got hit in the head."

She pushed out a thick plume of smoke. "It still could be a factor. The brain is sensitive. It likes to play, to create, to imagine. It never stops-- not even when we're sleeping. Any sort of trauma can affect it in some way."

"I just have this feeling she's not really a hallucination."

"You think she's real?"

"No . . ."

"Then why would you possibly think she's not-
-"

"She keeps popping up at the weirdest times."

"What does she do when she pops up?"

"Warns me about stuff. She's even gotten me out of trouble a couple of times."

"What's she warning you about?"

"The case I'm on."

"Why?"

"That's what I don't know."

"Ask her."

84

"I have."

"And what does she say?"

"She just disappears."

"Disappears? You mean she vanishes?"

"I just told you she pops up, didn't I? If she can pop up, she can also vanish. That's the reverse of popping up, isn't it? Pop up. Vanish."

Phil looked worried. I couldn't blame her. I was beginning to sound crazy. "Ralph, when you were hit in the head--"

"Like I said, I don't think it's that."

"You said you saw her before you were hit in the head."

"That's right."

"Did she pop up *before* you went into the men's room?"

"No . . ."

She shrugged. "See what I mean?"

"But when I first saw her--"

"She could've been a real person then, you know. A real person hiding from someone. You did say you'd seen her before . . . ."

That never occurred to me. "You know, you could be right."

"Maybe she actually ducked in there to hide from someone, and when you were hit--"

"Her image stayed in my head."

"If she was the last person you saw before you were knocked unconscious, it only makes sense that your brain caused her image to linger on."

85

"So she was real, but my blow to the head took her image, stuck it in there and did some really weird things to my perception of things."

Phil finished her cigarette and lit another. "A simple cut-and-paste by your brain might explain everything. How else could she manage the popping-up thing?"

"She couldn't. Not if she was real."

"Exactly."

"I'm glad I came here. You really do know how to figure out everything."

"Hardly."

"What do you mean? You just--"

"I can't figure out *everything*, Ralph. I'm still trying to understand why a man who hates fighting would find himself in one of the seediest places in Orlando."

"The case took me there."

"Of course it did."

"Besides, you can't get into a good fight at a snooty, high-brow place."

"Certainly not."

Her horns were beginning to show, but I knew better than leave it alone. What good was looking up your ex-wife if you didn't spend a little time sparring with her for old time's sake?

"They ask you to leave if you raise your voice, spill something or sneak a peek up a woman's skirt. They don't let you have any fun at all."

"I honestly didn't know that. I usually don't go to those so I can spill something on my expensive evening dress or peek up another woman's skirt."

"You really need to brush up on your society knowledge. There's a hierarchy when it comes to fighting in bars."

"I'm *so* glad you dropped by to tell me about it. I would never have known otherwise."

"I was in the neighborhood anyway, so . . ."

"You decided to give me a few hints that might come in handy for future events."

"Let's go with that."

"And to wrap up this unpleasantness at that Orlando dive, you went there on a case, stumbled upon a good-looking brunette in the men's room, then let someone use your head for a baseball."

"Why does it sound so stupid when you say it like that?"

"How am I supposed to say it?"

"I actually went into the dive to ask a few questions, stumbled upon the brunette and was suckered from behind."

"And this brunette--the one who was real at first but turned into a hallucination later on--warned you about this?"

"Just before I was suckered."

"That wasn't very nice. If she'd given you a little more warning--"

"I guess I might've gotten out of there in time if I hadn't been so shocked by her presence."

"Good point. And when did she show up again?"

"In the Emergency Ward, when they were pushing my brains back into my skull."

"And what did she say then?"

"She vanished before I could talk to her."

Phil nodded as though this actually made sense. "When did you see her again after that?"

"She came into Smilin' Susie's yesterday morning, while I was having breakfast."

"Why?"

"To see if I was all right."

"How sweet."

"I thought it was a nice gesture."

"Especially since she was just a hallucination and doesn't even know you."

"She's really good-looking, too."

"You've already mentioned that."

"I have?"

"Once or twice."

"I can't help it if I like good-looking women. I married one, didn't I?"

"Quit sucking up. It's so . . . beneath you."

"Sorry. I'll try really hard--*damn*!"

The brunette, dressed in a long-sleeve hunting shirt, jeans and white sneakers, materialized out of the corner of my eye.

"Ralph? You all right?"

"Is that your ex-wife?" the brunette whispered.

I didn't reply; I just nodded slightly.

"She's really beautiful," the brunette said.

"Ralph? You're pale."

I rubbed my eyes. My pulse hammered in my chest. The room had grown at least ten degrees warmer.

"Ralph?"

"My hallucination thinks you're beautiful."

88

"Really?"

"So far, she hasn't lied to me."

"Tell her thank you."

"I'm pretty sure she heard you."

Phil didn't reply.

I stopped rubbing my eyes. My vision cleared.

I found myself staring stupidly at the flower arrangement in the light-blue vase on the walnut table.

Chapter 10

Unnerved by what happened in Phil's office, I stopped by the Church Street Bar & Grill for a strong drink.

I had some Jack's in my desk drawer but didn't want to wait the half-hour it would take to fight traffic back to the office.

My waitress was about twenty-three, skinny and flat-chested, her long blond hair streaked with red and brown. Tattoos of barbed wire encircled both upper arms. *Sanchez* spanned the left side of her neck, *Duane* the right side. A large red rose embellished her bony cleavage. The word *Gorgeous,* printed lavishly in blue, accented the inside of her lower right arm. *Hot,* scrolled in red, adorned the inside of her lower left. Judging by her scowl and abrupt body movements, she was definitely upset about something. I wondered if Sanchez was giving her problems. Maybe it was Duane. Duane sounded more amiable, but you never knew nowadays. Prisons all over the country housed murderers, molesters and women-beaters named Duane. Probably a few Toby's, Marvin's and Purvis's tossed in there as well. You couldn't pick a name and come up with a feeling of genuine warmth these days.

It wasn't my business to ask, so I didn't.

She took my order and without a word stomped over to the bar to get my drink. While she was gone, I surveyed the room.

Half a dozen white-collared males just a year or two out of college sat at a table near the entrance. Two well-dressed women in their thirties occupied another table. A few sloppy-dressed tourists wandered around the dark, air-conditioned room, studying their surroundings as if they'd never seen a bar before.

A long-haired woman sat by herself about eight stools down, gazing into the bar mirror. She wore dress slacks and a long-sleeve white blouse. Her hair was curly and looked like it had spent a lot of time in a salon. I caught her glancing at me when my mean-faced waitress brought my double Jack's on ice.

The drink, thank God, was strong. I definitely needed it.

I tried coming to grips with what happened in Phil's office.

She showed up *there. In* Phil's office, *of all places. Showed up out of the blue, scaring the crap out of me, and in ten lousy seconds convinced Phil I was as loony as a bedbug.*

It made me realize that my visit to see Phil wasn't such a smart career move. It started out pretty well. Hell, we even made a little progress sorting out our differences. Minus a couple of tiny rough spots, it proved to be a pretty enjoyable ride.

Would've *stayed* that way, too--if my hallucination hadn't shown up.

I couldn't blame Phil for thinking I was crazy, or at least just a few steps short of certifiable. If the tables were turned, I'd probably think the same

91

thing. Phil had always suspected I had a few screws loose, but her suspicions were based on the fact that I preferred hunting down dangerous bad guys rather than sitting in someone else's office, listening to my arteries hardening. When you looked at things that way, you couldn't help thinking that seeing a professional shrink might not be such a bad idea.

The chick on the barstool glanced at me again.

I had another swig of Jack's and wondered if she was a genuine female or just another manifestation of my hallucination. If she was my hallucination, she certainly knew how to keep pushing the envelope.

It was too dark in the bar. I couldn't make out her face. The hair color was about right--black or dark-brown--and the right length. The bod fit as well. The outfit looked a little too fancy, but since my hallucination obviously enjoyed toying with me, changing her wardrobe frequently would be the perfect touch to keep me off my guard.

But why would she show up on a barstool?

Wouldn't she just pop up at my table? Or materialize in the seat next to me?

There was one sure way to nip this in the bud.

I strolled over to where she sat, sipping what looked like a strawberry daiquiri.

Hallucinations didn't drink, did they? But they also didn't use the phone.

"Hi."

"Hello," she said indifferently.

As I drew closer, I realized it wasn't her. But since I'd already started the ball rolling, I didn't know how to bow out of this without looking like a moron. The one sure thing about females: They all seemed to possess the natural ability to make any man look and feel stupid. And no matter how hard the guy fought it, he couldn't alter the end result.

I figured that on this rare occasion, honesty might work.

"I, uh, noticed you watching me."

No reply.

"You *were* watching me, weren't you?"

"I hadn't noticed."

"You didn't notice if you were watching me?"

"Not really." She slurped more of her drink through her straw. Then consulted her watch.

I wanted to tell her this wasn't an attempt to pick her up but knew better. That was the *one* thing you just didn't tell a woman--especially in a bar.

Women were experts at sexual games. They knew better than to help you out when you were acting stupid. It was something they knew by the time they were three years old. The more of an idiot a man makes of himself in their presence, the more superior a woman feels. That's why they never give you a clue when you're trying to pick them up. First of all, they truly enjoy the attention. They also don't want to coax the process along because it makes them look desperate.

But if they realize you *aren't* trying to pick them up, they go nuclear. *No* woman can tolerate a man who isn't attracted to them. They'll retaliate by turning him into stone--or a mass of quivering flesh--by any means possible.

In this case, I decided to just bow out gracefully. I turned to go back to my stool.

A man's deep voice resonated somewhere behind me.

"You okay, babe?" A huge square mass of flesh wrapped in an ill-fitting sports jacket stood behind the woman like a freestanding brick wall about to topple over.

I realized then that I should've kept my butt planted firmly to my stool.

"He thought I was watching him," the woman said flatly.

Silence.

"*Were* ya?"

"Of *course* not, darling," she cooed.

I knew I was toast.

"Wanna leave my wife alone?" The mass straightened, making itself a couple of inches taller--which it didn't need, since I only came up to its belt buckle. "Or do ya wanna settle this out in the parking lot?"

"Settle what?"

"You being a smartass?"

I wanted to tell him I couldn't be anything *but* a smartass even if I tried. But I knew saying that wouldn't exactly help my case. "Actually, leaving sounds like a pretty nifty idea."

"You're not as stupid as you look."

"Thank you."

I always thank someone when I'm complimented.

Kindness is so rare nowadays.

94

Chapter 11

I got back to my office a little after three and called Neil Haversack.

Neil was busy, so I left a message, sat back in my comfortable, ergonomically incorrect, hundred-dollar chair, and waited.

The double Jack's the tattooed lady gave me half an hour ago continued working on my nerves so I decided not to have another drink just yet. I was a little restless but too lazy to make a pot of coffee. That would require getting up, pouring water from the bathroom sink and filling the coffeepot. Entirely too much hustle and bustle for my present state of mind.

My harmonica would really come in handy about now. Sometimes playing it helped me unwind; other times it helped me think. Still other times, it helped me do both. But it never failed to relax me after a particularly stressful day.

I considered the last few hours pretty stressful. I'd wanted to play it more and more lately, but since I never knew if or when I was going to fall into the hands of sadistic crazies, I didn't want anyone taking it from me. If I'd had it when I went to Kelsey's, I might not have it any more. It was a high school graduation present from my father.

I firmly believed that if everyone played a musical instrument, there would be no violence or stress in the world.

While waiting to hear from Neil, I decided to tell him about my mysterious brunette. I knew that might be asking for trouble, but since this was bugging me so much, I really needed some professional input about what to do. Telling Phil about it surely didn't help. It might have if the brunette hadn't popped up.

But she had.

Like right now.

She stood in front of the door, wearing the same outfit she had on in Phil's office.

"Why'd you show up in my ex-wife's office?" I tried appearing more curious than angry but still ended up sounding abrupt and a little perturbed. I guess I could have used another slug or two of Jack's after all.

She shrugged. "Just curious."

"About what?"

"Your ex-wife."

"Why should you care?"

"I care a *lot*."

"Why? And why are you here? And who *are* you, by the way? And why do you look so damned *familiar*?"

"You sure do ask a lot of questions."

"Really? A gorgeous brunette pops up like magic and a guy isn't supposed to ask a slew of questions?"

"You think I'm gorgeous?" She tilted her head. Her hair slid down her arm.

I hated when women did that. It made a guy forget his name, what he was talking about--everything.

"You *really* think so?" she asked.

I shrugged. "A figure of speech."

"Then you *don't* think I'm gorgeous?"

"I wouldn't kick you out of bed . . ."

"Thank you. But I do care. It's why I'm here."

"*How's* that?"

"I came to warn you."

"*Warn* me?" I sat up sharply.

"You have five minutes."

"Until what?"

"Those guys you went to see last night?"

"I'm still trying to figure that one out. You never did say if you were the one who knocked on the door when--"

"Now you've got *four* minutes."

"That minute really went by *fast*."

"I'm serious, now."

"Listen. I'm expecting a call from my friend at OPD and--"

"They're on their way here, as we speak. And they're armed."

I spun my chair around. The heavy Orange Avenue traffic revealed nothing different or suspicious other than the usual solid streams of traffic. "How many?"

"Three. And they're all big and rough-looking. No offense . . ."

"I'm not very big. I know that. I don't need a daily reminder. My bathroom mirror is bad enough.

But at least I don't have to spend a fortune getting my clothes to fit so I don't look like an elephant hauling around a tent."

"I just meant these guys are *big*."

"I appreciate the warning."

"If I were you, I'd get out of here *now*."

I took another quick gander across the street. Smilin' Susie's did their usual booming early dinner business. The credit union next to it was busy. The tire shop and the oil change place also bustled. The fast food place at the end of the block swarmed with lines of cars. The 7-Eleven at the other end entertained its usual packed lot.

But no sign of three oversized morons in ill-fitting suits.

"Like I said, I appreciate the warning. But would you mind telling me who you are?"

No reply.

I spun my chair around.

She was gone.

***

I was sitting at my desk, the *Sentinel* opened in front of me, when the three of them stormed in.

Concealed by the paper, my .380 Beretta Cheetah filled my right hand. The safety was off, the hammer cocked, the slab barrel aimed at the door.

The goon in the rear, a doorman at the club, closed the door quietly and stood blocking it, his arms crossed over his huge barrel chest. Just as he did in front of Vesper's. If he had a personalized card to give to his friends and acquaintances, it would probably say something like:

> MY NAME IS GODZILLA
> I BLOCK DOORS
> *(no door too big!)*

The other two approached my desk--one from the right, the other from the left. Lou the barman stopped a few feet to my left. The other guy, some ape I'd never seen before, complemented the picture of Neanderthal bookends.

If I tilted the barrel of the .380 an inch to the right, I'd get Godzilla even with my bad aim. Six inches in either direction would nail Lou or Ape Number Two. But I had to be careful. If I was even a little off, this shindig would turn into something I didn't even want to think about.

"You guys taking a well-deserved break?" I asked pleasantly. "Get a little bored with luring customers away from the dancers and suckering them?"

"Funny," Lou said.

I turned to the other guy. "You the gentleman with the strange pillowcase fixation?"

"Howzat?"

"You've got a thing for pillowcases. Like Linus and his blanket, only you're older, not cute, but *much* more psychotic."

"Who the fuck's *Linus*?"

"You know, you really ought to see a specialist about that. It probably has something to do with your mother not being around much when you were an infant. Or maybe you weren't breast-fed. I can recommend a good psychiatrist. She'd have a ball with someone of your, uh, mental incapacities."

He frowned--possibly because he had no idea what I just said. It took him a little while to discover he'd just been insulted. "You talk tough for an asshole whose face is about to be rearranged."

"You don't like my face the way it is?"

His frown turned into a grin. It wasn't pretty. I preferred the frown. It made him look less stupid. The grin made him appear goofy and slightly drunk.

"I think we might be able to improve a little on it," he said.

"My mother would disagree with you on that."

"Let's not bring Mommy into this, yeah?"

"See there? I *knew* you had a thing against mothers."

Pillowcase's frown came back. "Listen, asshole--"

I shrugged. "So where's your pillowcase? You guys don't know how to work on anyone who's watching you, do you?"

"Sure we do," Pillowcase said without thinking.

"Can it," Lou growled.

"So now there are *three* of you," I said amiably. "I'm actually honored."

"You're asking for it." Lou took a step closer.

"What the hell's he *honored* for?" Pillowcase frowning again.

"Shuddup." Lou made a move for his jacket pocket.

I let the paper drop. The .380 pointed directly at his face.

Lou froze. Gorilla dropped his arms. Pillowcase gasped and stepped back.

"Now that I've got your attention. . . ." I made a mental note to thank my lovely hallucination the next time she popped up. "You caught me off-guard before, but I was out of my element. Get your hand away from that pocket."

Lou lowered his hand to his side. "You wouldn't shoot us." The doubt hung heavy in his voice.

"You don't think so?"

He forced a smirk. "Little shit like you? Don't have it in you."

"You steal money from a customer, blind him with a pillowcase, then sucker him with a slam to the gut and you don't think he'll shoot you the first chance he gets? You have a lot to learn about human nature." I waited for that to sink in. When I saw the color draining from his face I added, "If you want to call my bluff, go right ahead. Take a step closer. You might get lucky. But I honestly don't think I can miss at this distance."

He didn't move.

"You. Godzilla." I gestured toward the square slab of muscle blocking the door. "Get over here and stand beside your keeper."

His small square forehead wrinkled.

"In plain English, that means your friend Lou."

He lumbered over and took his place beside the barman.

"Pillowcase, go over to Godzilla and complete the picture of indiscriminate inbreeding."

"Wh-*What*--"

"Sorry. My wit's sometimes a tad sophisticated for the less-educated crowd. Get over there with Curly and Larry."

He reluctantly joined the group.

Godzilla glared at me. He obviously wanted to do something heroic but was nervous about the gun pointed directly at his sixty-inch chest. I honestly hoped he wouldn't move. I didn't think someone his size would go down from just one .380 slug and I sure didn't want to empty the clip and sit there like a shithead, waiting for Lou and Pillowcase to finish me off.

Godzilla said, "I don't take no fucking orders from no--"

"Zip it." I sat up. My gun didn't waver. I was really surprised how calm I was. I wanted to analyze it so I could do it again later on but figured this wasn't a real good time. Maybe later, if I managed to get out of this in one piece.

The phone rang. The threesome cringed.

"Dammit. Just when I was beginning to enjoy myself."

Lou said, "Listen here, Deacon--"

"Grab some sky."

Total confusion set in again.

"Doesn't anyone watch Westerns anymore? Raise your hands."

Slowly they raised their hands.

I kept the gun trained and picked up the receiver. "I'm kind of busy right now, so this better be good."

It was Neil. "I just got your message. What's happening?"

"Right now I'm having one hell of an office party. It isn't my birthday, but I'm apparently the guest of honor. It's a casual come-as-you-are thing. Problem is, the three idiots here came as they are and they're just as stupid now as they were when they got here."

"Deacon, what the hell's going on?"

"Doesn't anyone understand English anymore? Oh. That's right--this is Florida. All sorts of foreign tongues to contend with. Listen . . . I've got my gun trained on three gorillas who work at Vesper's. They tried sneaking in on me."

"You *what*?"

"What part of that didn't come through?"

"You're *serious*?"

"As serious as always. Want to send some men over to pick them up? I haven't patted them down. I thought I'd let your guys earn their money. I've got the strangest feeling these boys might be packing."

Lou's face had paled. "Listen, Deacon, we just came here to--to *talk* . . ."

"Shut up."

"What's that?" Neil said.

"One of my party guests just tried apologizing for their come-as-you-are apparel but it sounds

103

pretty lame. Since they were the ones who organized this shindig, I think they should've shown up as gorgeous blondes. Or maybe two blondes and a striking redhead. I'd even settle for a mysterious brunette."

A heavy sigh. "Deacon, are you gonna swear out a complaint?"

"Sure. Why not? It's trespassing, isn't it?"

"I thought this was a *business*," Lou said sourly.

"It usually is. But my potential clients normally don't come in here, guard the door, threaten me with on-the-spot facial surgery, then reach into their pocket to pull out a gun. That *is* a gun you were going for, isn't it, Lou?"

"Deacon?" Neil sounded impatient.

"How can I help you, Neil?"

"You called *me*, remember?"

"That's right. The party thing. Can you do something about this? I honestly don't think they came here to obtain my professional services." I looked at Lou. "You don't need a private detective for anything right now, do you?"

Lou flinched. "What the fuck are you--"

"I didn't think so. I was right, Neil. They aren't on the premises to obtain my professional services. Just the facial surgery, I imagine. I guess that means loitering. Is there such a thing as armed loitering?"

"All right, all right. We'll haul them in and see what we can come up with. A simple weapons charge might be all it takes to get them off the street for an hour or so."

"Can you pick them up fairly quickly? I don't know how much longer I can keep my gun on them without my wrist cramping up. Old war injury."

"*What* war? You're too young for Nam and I don't remember you volunteering for Saudi."

Sometimes Neil could be downright irritating. "Just call it early-stage arthritis and get a couple of uniforms here, all right?"

Chapter 12

Neil Haversack, a big, burly man with blond hair cut to a light stubble and broad, rosy cheeks, was the sort of cop you'd expect to see on a beat, twirling his nightstick.

But right now, he appeared tired and a little under the weather. His light-blue eyes were blood-shot; the dark puffs beneath them gave him a paler complexion than usual. Neil was a worrier. He was also a workaholic--which explained the blood-shot eyes and the tired, pale appearance.

But something else was bothering him. He'd been staring at me suspiciously since I walked into the building. I had the strange feeling I'd done something wrong even though on this rare occasion I knew I hadn't. At first I thought I'd tracked something in. I did what anyone else would do under the same circumstances--I checked my shoes.

"Step in something?" he asked.

"One can never be too careful."

"Deacon, once again you're making no sense whatsoever."

"Why spoil my perfect record?"

"We certainly wouldn't want *that*."

"Can't help it."

"Help what?"

"Being paranoid. You're looking at me funny."

"*Funny*?"

"Like those motel people when you check out."

"And how's *that*?"

106

"Suspicious. But I didn't take anything. Honest. I just came in."

"But I *am* suspicious."

"Is it because you're wondering how I managed to get the drop on those three?"

Neil nodded. "You've gotten pretty good at mind-reading."

I shrugged. It seemed the perfect time to summon my fabrication skills. "I was just lucky. What else can I say? My gun was out. I was admiring it."

"Admiring your gun. Hmmm . . ." He gave me one of his world-weary, tired-cop expressions. "Are we still talking firearms here? Or are you slipping in a sexual innuendo for some ridiculous reason?"

"Me? Ridiculous?"

"I know, I know. What was I thinking? Let's get on with this while we're both still relatively young enough to keep our attention on the subject."

"Like I said, my gun was out. Occasionally I take it out, check the clip and swap out the bullets."

"Sounds reasonable so far."

"Anyway, they came in at the wrong time. I'd just snapped the clip back in and put the gun in my lap. They barged right in and looked at me funny. Not the way *you* were just looking at me, though. More of a sinister, Russian-Mob-type flavor. Like when Goldfinger glared at Bond at the country club right after Bond pulled that ball switcheroo on him."

"Goldfinger, I believe, was German."

"Whatever. Getting back to my story . . . I was still pissed about them suckering me earlier, so I was ready for them. And I wasn't in the mood for a funny look."

"That's it?"

"What else can I say? My biorhythm's on the upswing. The universe blipped. I have a guardian angel looking after me."

Neil was still having trouble with all this, going by the way he'd crinkled his face and scratched the back of his neck. "I'll buy the angel part."

"Really?" That floored me because it was the only thing I'd said that was even remotely close to the truth.

"Beats everything else you've said."

"It's impossible to sneak into a place when the guy inside knows you're coming in."

"And how would you know *that*?"

"I got a hot tip."

"From who?"

"If I told you, I'd lose him as an informant."

Neil didn't respond. Cops usually stopped the third degree when you mentioned informants. Just about every cop I knew used one. Nowadays, you couldn't work without them. Too much going on these days. No cop could survive or do his work effectively without having some sort of snitch on his payroll.

"That tip must've been sizzling," he finally said.

"Hot enough to coax me into taking out my gun."

I followed him down the hall, where the interview rooms lined the other end of the building. We passed a coffee station. Three pots of burnt coffee sat smoking quietly, anxiously waiting to clear up someone's sinuses or provide them with a new ulcer. I'd wanted a pick-me-up but cops seem to be unable to make good coffee, and anyhow I wanted to get this over with so I could get back to the apartment, have a warm shower and relax with a strong drink. I also wanted to play my harmonica and listen to some classic jazz later on. After a rough day, Miles, Coltrane or Chet Baker really did the trick. If the day was particularly taxing, no one worked better than Louis Armstrong. A mild day would require something from my big band collection. Although I hadn't had many of them, a terrific day would be shared with a woman, with Brubeck or Henry Mancini serenading us softly from the stereo.

A big cop with a shaved head stood guard outside the first interview room. The window displayed a bright, empty room.

"Where'd everyone go?" Neil asked the guard.

"Released."

I couldn't believe it. "Already?"

"How long ago?" Neil asked.

"Just a few minutes."

"I didn't even have a chance to have a cup of *coffee* yet." Not that I really *wanted* one, of course. But my irritation level required a little distraction.

"Who handled it?" Neil asked.

"Their fancy attorney showed up, handed over a chunk of cash and told us all to have a nice day."

Neil frowned at me. "That's some seriously heavy-duty legal representation."

"The kind the mob pays for."

"Is there something you're not telling me?" he asked.

"Not that I'm aware of."

"This was a simple strong-arm thing, wasn't it?"

I knew exactly what Neil was getting at. Those three had come to my office to scare me off the case or worse. But why? And who'd paid them?

Would a small-time crook like Don Brandon have that much money or clout? Even if he did, would he go to such extremes just to get out of paying some back child support?

"You know something, Neil? I'm beginning to wonder."

"It does seem a tad heavy-handed, doesn't it? Three big guys? Showing up in your office? In broad daylight? "

"There did seem to be an aura of negative urgency oozing from the threesome."

"Huh?"

"They all seemed pissed."

"Ah."

We went back to the coffee station. Neil poured two cups. I took the one he offered but promised my protesting stomach not to drink too much. I topped it off with four sugars and two creamers. It stayed black.

"Tell me about this case," Neil said.

"Not much to it. Don Brandon. Deadbeat dad. Three years behind in child support."

Neil sipped the scalding coffee. "And he's involved with the three that just walked out?"

"I went to Vesper's last night. Brandon's ex told me he goes there a lot. The three who came to see me are probably his drinking buds."

"What happened at Vesper's?"

"I almost got rolled."

"Almost?"

Time to start doing the old eggshell walk again. "I managed to get away before my muggers could have too much fun."

Neil shook his head. "Your biorhythm must be on a *giant* upswing."

"Timing can make or break a private eye." I tried not to sound too cocky.

"You're not serious."

I had a tiny sip. It burned my tongue, the roof of my mouth and the back of my throat on its way down. It also tasted just as bad as it smelled.

When I recovered, I said, "When have you ever known me not to be serious?"

"Just every time you open your mouth."

"It's an affliction I've had since I was a kid. When you're small, you need to compensate."

"For what?"

"Being small."

"I'd think being a smartass would get you in even *more* trouble."

"The bullies were busy trying to figure out what I'd told them. I was usually three blocks away before they realized what I'd actually meant."

"That *worked*?"

"Until I met up with a bully carrying around a brain cell."

"How often did *that* happen?"

"Not very, fortunately." It was time to go back to the office. When you just had three scary morons hauled in, you had to decide if they were mad enough to retaliate. "I guess I'll be leaving. It seems my work is done."

"You just might want to stay in close touch."

"How's that?"

"After all this, I'd say someone's definitely got a hard-on against you."

I decided to shrug it off. At least, while talking to Neil. You didn't want it to get out that you were actually *scared* of anyone. Not if you wanted to continue running a successful detective agency. Anyway, it was unmanly.

"They were trespassing," I said.

"You got their asses hauled in. They won't like that."

"They probably spent ten minutes, tops, in this building. All that did was interrupt their workday. I even saved them from a possible malpractice suit."

"A *what*?"

"Cosmetic surgery without a valid license or patient approval. They should appreciate the fact that they're off the hook."

"Let me know." He waved as he took his coffee back to his office.

"Let you know what?"

"When they try and kill you again."

"If I'm not too busy doing other important stuff," I said casually.

Tonight, Satchmo would definitely be needed.

Chapter 13

I could tell something was wrong as soon as I parked the TransAm and went up the walk to my garden apartment.

Private eyes--especially good ones--possess a sixth sense about such things. They can sniff the air and know something is different. Their eye will catch something out of place--the welcome mat shifted slightly or an unfamiliar vehicle parked where it's not supposed to be. They might even catch remnants of someone's aftershave drifting over from the palmettos or hear an almost inaudible rustling in the bushes when there is no breeze.

Thanks to the hallucinations I'd been having the last couple of days, I'd grown particularly sensitive to the set order of my immediate surroundings.

In this particular case, my front door was ajar.

I'd passed the bug guy's van on my way to my apartment--which told me it was his day to spray. But since he'd always been good about closing the door when he was finished and since the complex manager usually followed him around to make sure everything was secure, there was no reason for my door to be open.

Unless, of course, someone else was inside.

I always lock my door. You really have to. In my profession, you do and say things a lot of the wrong people don't like. Even if you're not a detective, you don't want to leave your door unlocked.

In Florida, where people from all over the world are wandering around, trying to figure out where everything is, everyone is suspicious. The meter reader. The kid selling magazine subscriptions. Anyone can buy a uniform at a costume shop and gain access to apartments and condos while the occupants are at work or visiting the theme parks.

I found this out through years of experience as a private eye.

And by watching *Monk* reruns.

But today I was especially on my guard. The incident in my office--as well as the trip to OPD and my talk with Neil--had spooked me. I probably checked my rearview mirror more than a dozen times during the short trip back home. I promised myself I'd take no chances. Looking like a paranoid nutcase was a lot better than ending up dead.

I got out the Beretta and held it against the side of my leg. With my free hand I gently nudged the door forward a few inches. Then slipped through the opening.

The silence mocked me. Faint bug poison residue languished in the flow of the air-conditioning. I silently went down the hall and carefully checked the bedroom, the closet and underneath the bed, then began a meticulous search for strange wires and small metal boxes. I went through my dresser drawers and then examined the drawers of the end table and the inside of the small walnut jewelry case Phil bought me one year for my birthday. I inspected my box springs. Then I went into the bathroom, picked up the porcelain lid behind the bowl and looked inside.

I spent the next ten minutes in the kitchen, checking cabinets, the fridge and the broom closet. I also looked at the hot water heater and the air conditioning unit.

Nothing.

But I couldn't shake the feeling that someone had been in my apartment.

Someone other than the bug guy.

I left the apartment and went down the concrete walk behind the pool that cut across the heart of the complex. A couple of teen boys screamed as they tossed each other in the water. Two bikini-clad teen girls sat in lounge chairs, egging them on.

The bug guy's truck was parked along the curb outside the L-shaped building that served as the office, supply room and recreation area. The bug guy, tall and wiry, with huge wet circles under the arms of his light-blue uniform and beads of sweat streaking his tanned cheeks, had nearly finished reeling in the long hose he used on the grass.

"Hey, Joe." The name on his pocket said *JOE*, so that's what I called him.

He nodded and waved.

A healthy mix of B.O. and bug spray drifted my way in the heavy early evening heat. I decided to make this brief. "Remember doing the J building?"

He nodded.

116

"Remember closing all the doors?"

"Always do."

"Every one of them?"

"Abso-damn-lutely."

"You sure?"

"Get fired if I don't."

"See anyone hanging around?"

He squinted--possibly to understand the question better.

"Someone big and stupid-looking, maybe?" I figured a little more detail might help jog something loose. Specifics usually help people visualize easier.

He chuckled. "Sounds like most of my drinkin' buddies."

I guess I needed to be even *more* specific. "I meant hanging around J Building. Near my door? Maybe wearing a suit?"

"A *suit*?" He scratched the back of his neck.

I was obviously speaking a foreign language. "You know. Jacket? Tie? Pressed slacks? Good shoes?"

For a moment he looked like he wanted to laugh. He just shook his head.

I went back to my apartment. My bottle of Jack Daniel's remained where I'd left it on the kitchen counter. I wasn't going to hesitate draining it.

On my way back to the armchair I picked up the remote and flicked it on. HG TV instantly came on with the Garden Guy. Good deal. A program with plants, birds and trimmed trees might relax me.

I liked this channel. It was quiet and comfortable. Almost like golf. Or those shows with the fancy-dressed dudes on horses jumping over fences.

On the screen, the Garden Guy explained a safe way to rid your garden of wasps.

Garden Guy really knew his shit about gardens. If I ever had the chance to have a garden, I'd definitely buy every DVD he ever made.

I drained my glass, then got back up and checked the apartment again.

Still nothing.

So why couldn't I shake the nagging feeling that someone had been here?

Was it because of what happened in my office earlier?

Or because I was worried about what Neil had told me about those dudes wanting to retaliate?

Probably both.

In any event, I intended to keep my guard up to the critical level.

At least until I found Brandon.

I poured two inches more of Jack's, drained it in one swallow and watched the Garden Guy and another show, this one about raising earthworms.

After a couple of home renovation shows, I thought about trying to sleep. I made sure the chain was on the door and the deadbolt pushed in all the way before I turned off all the lights and got ready for bed.

Before I got into bed, I consulted my CD collection to help me relax.

Satchmo lay three down from the top, waiting patiently for me to slide him into the player.

Chapter 14

The next morning, I stepped out of the shower, toweled off and set about scraping off the fresh growth covering my face.

I still hadn't washed my hair because of my goose egg. I didn't want to chance upsetting it and delaying the healing process.

After splashing my cheeks with *Stetson* and carefully combing my hair, I checked out my reflection.

At least I looked better than the day before. My color had returned. And the half-dead eyes staring back at me in the bathroom mirror the night before appeared much more focused.

The kitchen phone rang. It was Phil.

"Hear more voices lately?"

"Actually, I'm hearing one now."

"I'm serious."

This probably wasn't the right time to tell her that my hallucination had visited my office yesterday afternoon and saved my life.

"So am I," I said. "Can't you hear the sincerity singing from this voice?"

"You must be joking."

"The question was rhetorical anyway."

"Ralph, you came to my office looking like you just crawled away from a train wreck. Don't tell me I'm supposed to forget about that."

One of Phil's most irritating flaws--she didn't forget anything. But then, most of the women I'd known, including my mother, possessed that same flaw. I figured it was a common trait that came as a sort of package deal with the estrogen gene.

"Well?" She obviously didn't want me wasting too much time thinking up a dynamite answer. "Tell me how I'm supposed to be treating this."

I'd hoped she'd think it was some sort of memory blip on my part, possibly due to my tap to the head. Phil had seen me at my worst before. And since she hated what I did for a living, she'd probably be more than eager to blame my hallucination on my head injury. The fact that my hallucination had materialized during our visit might even have convinced her more than ever that my concussion was responsible.

"Just forget about it. You know how I am."

"I've also seen the latest lump on your head."

"Meaning?"

"You involve yourself with vicious, sociopathic people who need to be in prison."

"Nobody's perfect."

"Ralph . . ."

"Besides, everyone has accidents."

"Being shot at, hit by a moving car and knocked senseless doesn't happen to everyone."

"When I was knocked senseless?"

"Besides the other night?"

"I don't count that one."

"Why not?"

"It's too recent."

"You're taking this very lightly."

"It's a new day. Look how the morning started. I got a phone call from a beautiful woman who's truly concerned about my health and well-being."

"Can't you be serious when you're supposed to be?"

"Tell me when I'm supposed to be and I'll try."

"Right now would be lovely."

"Sometimes you want things to be too easy. Cut and dried. Open and shut."

I heard her sighing. "Ralph, you're pushing it."

"Pushing what?"

"My patience."

"Well, it's not like I haven't done *that* before . . ."

"This isn't the right time for it. You showed up yesterday afternoon with that huge lump on the back of your head and your story about a mysterious brunette popping up. Then she apparently popped up in my office, told you I was beautiful, then vanished."

"You *are* beautiful."

"Stop changing the subject."

I decided to try the innocent approach. It wasn't exactly my strong point but it was worth a shot. "You know I do that frequently when I'm at a loss for words."

"Do *what* frequently? And just when are you at a loss for words?"

That was something else that always irritated me about women--you had to explain everything to them. They couldn't just belch and say, yup, nope or I hear what you're saying, dude--like guys did when they got together to drink and act stupid.

"It's this case I'm working on. I've been under a lot of stress--"

"I know. We used to be married, remember?"

"Vaguely."

"Asshole."

"A woman never forgets those cherished pet names, does she?"

"Seriously, are you okay now? I'm worried about you."

"Like I said, it's this case I'm on."

"What's it about?"

"Well, my client has been having trouble with her ex and--"

"Nice-looking?"

"Her ex?"

"Your *client,* silly."

"I guess so."

"Stacked?"

"How'd you come up with *that*?"

"Ralph, you've always acted silly and brainless around stacked women."

"I acted silly and brainless around you, too."

"I'm not stacked."

It never ceased to amaze me how often she chose to remind me of that even though one glance was all it took to show me she wasn't.

"Your breast size was never an issue."

Silence.

I knew she liked that. But being the masochistic idiot that I was, I couldn't leave it alone.

"Your height was my only genuine concern. But I was only concerned for your sake."

"I clearly remember *that* excuse."

"You insist on wearing those platform wedgies that make you eight feet tall. Any guy who isn't a basketball player would look silly next to you."

"Ralph . . ."

"I know. Water under the dam."

"Over the bridge."

"Whatever."

"So you're all right, then? Seriously?"

"Reasonably."

"Please take care of yourself. I mean that. Sincerely."

After a breakfast of bacon, eggs, toast and coffee, I decided that since my hallucination--as well as my intruders the day before--had told me the opposition knew what I looked like, I ought to try another tactic. I slipped into my Joe Tourist disguise--Hawaiian shirt, Bermuda shorts, tennis shoes and my old Detroit Tigers baseball cap. I found a Triple-A Orlando map, a cheap disposable camera in my dresser and a pair of wraparound sunglasses I hadn't worn in ages. I had a brown paste-on Buffalo Bill mustache that made me look like Al Pacino in one of his street-hood roles if the light hit me a certain way. However, anyone could tell I'm not him even though our hair is similar. I'm much taller, I'm proud to say--at least six inches, possibly seven. Our voices and accents don't match--which doesn't mean anything. In Florida, everyone speaks a different language. No one pays much attention to one another, anyway.

I had to leave my gun. Tourists don't carry guns. At least, not that I know of.

I needed complete anonymity. I planned to check out Vesper's again, this time as your plain, ordinary Joe away from the wife and kids, visiting a place where he could drink and act stupid.

But based on my prior experiences with the place, I had to be extra careful. Vesper's meant Mob . . . which meant big-time drug distributors . . . which meant Miami . . . which meant Raguzzo.

According to the scuttlebutt, Old Man Raguzzo left Miami in the late nineties and now lived in an exclusive area in Central Florida, still operating as actively as ever. He liked using family and also liked spreading his organization outward. It gave him more control and helped feed his ego, which was legendary. He employed local muscleheads because they were easy to find on the beaches and in the gyms. They were stupid, didn't ask questions, worked cheaply and were eager to flex whenever the situation required it.

The doormen at Vesper's were undoubtedly hand-picked by Raguzzo. This told me I should have my head examined for even considering going back there.

But I'd had my head examined before.

It never revealed anything that mattered that much.

Chapter 15

At 12:05, Vesper's parking lot was nearly half-filled even though most of their lunch crowd hadn't arrived yet.

I parked the rented tan Nissan in the first vacant space I could find. Suspecting someone would remember the TransAm, I switched vehicles in one of the rental places on South Semoran to complete my Joe Tourist adventure.

I wandered up the concrete path, taking pictures. I knew they'd confiscate the camera at the door, but a tourist wouldn't know their policy and I didn't want to blow my clueless image. My Pirates cap was pushed way up in front and down in back to conceal the bandage. At least my goose egg had shrunk a little. It was still tender, but I'd be fine as long as I gave it time to heal and kept it away from pistol butts and leather saps.

One of the two steroid brutes instantly blocked me from getting within twenty feet of the doorway. He did a dandy job, too. He also blocked the door, most of the building, the woods behind him and the Florida Turnpike exit ramp half a mile beyond the tree line.

"No cameras," he said in an irritated monotone.

"Why not?"

"Club policy." The other doorman held out an open palm. It was as big as one of those platters Denny's uses for their breakfast specials.

"Explain it to me," I said.

"Huh?"

"The policy."

He took another step toward me until my nose almost touched his ribcage. I felt both fear and instant security. In the event of a sudden tropical rainstorm, his chest would keep my entire body dry. He looked down and scowled. "You don't give me the camera? You don't get in. Get it?"

"I feel *so* much better since you've explained the policy in such detail," I told his stomach.

The huge platter of flesh remained held out.

I handed it over. "Do I get it back when I come back out?"

He closed his hand. The camera disappeared. "Sure."

"The film, too?"

"Sure." He just didn't sound convincing. Good thing it only cost me eight bucks.

"Ten bucks, cover," the first one said.

I pulled the slender wad from my pocket and gave him two fives. "You weren't *that* bad in *Predator*," I said.

He just nodded. He obviously didn't catch the insult.

Idiots were *so* much fun to play with.

They both stepped aside and let me walk through the open door.

Being a glutton for punishment, I decided to go back to where I found trouble during my last visit. I went down the hall and followed the lap dancing signs.

126

The room was just as hectic as always. The men paying for the dancers all looked the same-- thirty, well-dressed, thin and clean-shaven, with buzz cuts--and all wore the same sweaty expressions as they continuously fed bills to their dancer.

Lou wasn't at the bar. The present barman, tall and broad-shouldered, looked fit but obviously wasn't a juiced-up bodybuilder. Apparently Vesper's occasionally hired normal-looking barmen. I decided to have a drink and see what I could find out.

"I'll have a Guinness."

He was only gone a few moments, returning with my beer in a frosted mug.

"How's the action here?"

"You don't look local." His reply told me he might actually be carrying around a brain cell or two.

"I'm not. How's the action here?"

"Where you from?" He glanced at my cap. "Detroit?"

"Good guess."

He nodded, pleased with himself. Like I said, idiots are fun to play with. Even idiots with a brain cell. "You down here with the wife and kids?"

I had a slug of ice-cold Guinness. "You got it."

"You escaped to come here, right?"

I had more Guinness. "What was your first clue? The cap? The sunglasses?"

"The fake stash."

My defenses instantly climbed into high gear. I glanced around the room. No one creeping up behind me. Luckily, everyone was obsessed with the sweaty, nearly naked dancers and could care less about a messy-looking male tourist wearing a fake Buffalo Bill. "How do you know it's fake?"

"It don't match."

"I color it."

"The stash?"

"The hair."

"Listen here, sport." He lowered his voice. "I do hair when I'm not fixing drinks. That's definitely fake. Ten bucks, tops."

"I'll have you know--"

"If you paid more than ten, they saw you coming."

"There's no way you can tell--"

"Want me to rip it off?"

"You'd look awfully silly if you were wrong. And you'd lose the huge tip I planned to give you."

"One way to find out for sure."

"I'm not really into pain, so I guess you win." I had more Guinness. Time to change the subject. "So where do you do hair?"

He puffed up a little. "Got a small place at a strip mall north off of Orange, couple blocks from Michigan. Stop by, I'll sell you a stash no one can spot. What're you wearing it for? Want some action?"

"You *are* good."

He suddenly frowned. "You ain't a cop, are you?"

"Do I look like one?"

He squinted. "You're kinda small."

"I'm five-eleven." I straightened on my stool and tried looking taller and more menacing--which is kind of difficult in a messy tourist disguise.

"Not much meat on you, though."

"I consider myself wiry."

He chuckled as if he'd just heard a nasty joke. I wanted to toss the Guinness in his face, climb up his tie and poke out his eyeballs. But I decided to forgive him. He was providing me information.

"So why the fake stash?"

"I like the tables--especially blackjack. The wife turns into a banshee if she thinks I'm playing."

He nodded. Guys become instant buddies when women are involved. You don't have to say much at all to gain another guy's sympathy. Just let him know about your wife or temperamental girlfriend. He'll practically turn into Doctor Phil on you.

"I heard there are some high-stakes games going on here."

He jabbed a thumb at the hall behind him. "Follow the sign that says Games."

"I figured that was for something else."

"That's the idea. Cops come in, the section's automatically blocked off and they end up looking like shitheads. Nothing but foosball, pinball, pool and video games out in front."

"Clever."

"It's a good system. Why fix it if it ain't broke?"

"You've got a point."

"Go on, have yourself a ball. Got money?"

"I'm good."

A grin. "Got *lots* of money?"

"Actually, I'm a retired millionaire." I dropped a ten on the counter.

"That sounds like bullshit."

"How could you tell?"

"Rich jerks don't tip."

"Good catch." I slid off the stool and went down the hall past the men's room, several pay phones and three doors. One was marked *Games*, one *Manager* and the last one unmarked.

The unmarked door cracked open as soon as I passed. Before another heavy dose of *déjà vu* could wash over me, something that felt suspiciously like a gun barrel poked me roughly between the shoulder blades.

Instinctively I raised my hands, but a harsh whisper close behind me said, "Lower your fucking arms, asshole."

I did so.

"Now back up."

"Where?"

"Just shut up and do it."

"How far? I don't walk too well backward. Ruins my balance. I suffer from vertigo and a ringing in the ears."

"Shut up and back up until I say stop, dumbass."

I backed up until darkness engulfed me. I was about to ask what was going on when the pressure on my back disappeared. Instinct told me to duck or turn my head. I started to turn but only managed to move a few inches to my left before a cloth dipped in something sweet and reeking of medicine covered my face.

I lashed out, but grogginess came quickly.

Then blackness.

Chapter 16

Something large and bony slapped me across the face.

My head throbbed, but the hot pain dancing across my cheeks made me quickly forget about what was going on anywhere else.

I opened my eyes.

The huge semi-dark room looked like some sort of warehouse. Long, thick slices of bright light cut in through the oblong windows near the roof, forming hazy bars on the concrete floor beside me. Two gleaming stretch limos stood beside one another about thirty feet off to my left. Behind them, a shiny Ferrari sat by itself. Against a far wall, long rows of boxes stacked on palettes reached halfway to the rafters. The heavy reek of gas and oil singed my nostrils.

I sat in a metal chair, my wrists fastened to the arms by those sharp plastic zip-ties the cops use. The ties were pulled tight. My hands tingled from lack of circulation.

My tennies were gone. So was my Tigers cap. The concrete floor, smooth and ice-cold on my bare feet, made me shiver. My naked ankles, similarly zip-tied to the metal legs of the chair, also tingled.

The figure standing in front of me, tall and broad-shouldered, wore a loose-fitting gray sweatshirt and black sweatpants. His head covered with a black hood. The eyes behind the jagged slits in the material were dark and slightly blood-shot. I tried to remember what color Lou's eyes were. My head was too cloudy. And I was too nervous at the moment to concentrate.

"Start talking," the hooded man whispered.

I suspected he was speaking softly so I wouldn't recognize his voice. I'd probably seen him in the club. He could be the hair guy tending bar.

"I think I must have been slightly misunderstood in the lap dancing room."

"*What*?"

"I came here to play *blackjack*--not indulge in a little S & M. And if I *wanted* to indulge, it would be with a chick. Sorry, but you ain't no chick."

I figured he might appreciate a little sharp wit under the circumstances. You know--some healthy admiration for someone who could look adversity in the eye and still keep a firm upper lip.

I figured wrong.

This slap, harder than its predecessor, nearly upset my chair. Hot waves of jagged pain scraped down my chest and arms like loose strands of barbed wire.

"I can do this all day, smartass."

That was a lie if I ever heard one. How could anyone spend the day slapping someone in the face without getting bored? But I didn't say anything because I'd probably get slapped again. I just sat quietly and waited for the waves to ebb.

When you're faced with a tense situation like this one, your mind tries to bail. It's like some higher power telling you that you were a dumbass for getting yourself into this and much too stupid to get out of it on your own.

Your mind first tries to convince you that you're not really here. You're imagining this. You might even be dreaming it. When you open your eyes, you'll find yourself in your bedroom. If that doesn't work, you can expect the guy hurting you to pull off his hood and yell, "April Fool!" or "Just kidding!" He'll cut you loose and tell you to get out and never come back.

If the situation is *really* tense, your mind might even convince you that you're a kid again. You never grew up in the first place. Your imagination has cooked this up. Too many action movies. Too many suspense and espionage novels.

When I opened my eyes, the same huge, big-knuckled hand that had just slapped me held my fake mustache just inches in front of my face. "You came for blackjack, why the disguise?"

"Like I told the hair guy, my wife doesn't want me to gamble."

I watched in horror as he dropped my twenty-dollar mustache onto the dirty floor and mashed it with an enormous tennis shoe. When he shifted his weight, a metal stand appeared a few feet behind him. A variety of large, sinister-looking tools hung from it. A large ball-peen hammer, machete, screwdriver, pliers and other familiar-looking objects. All innocuous-looking under normal circumstances, but scary and menacing to me right now. Hannibal Lecter, serial killers and several of those nauseating *Saw* movies instantly came to mind.

"What's the problem?" I asked. "I brought money with me."

"Problem is we don't believe you."

"I brought a hundred bucks with me . . ."

"That's not what we're talking about."

"Then what *are* you--"

"You've been here before."

"Vesper's doesn't like repeat customers?"

"Not the kind wearing disguises and asking stupid questions."

He picked up the ball-peen hammer from his collection, dragged over a metal folding chair and sat facing me. He placed the hammer upright on the floor between my feet.

Since I was both observant and pessimistic, I had the feeling something extremely painful was about to happen.

"You like movies?"

Of course I like movies. I've been a fan all my life. In fact, I love them. But when someone knocks you out, ties you to a chair, picks up a ball-peen hammer and asks if you like movies, your first reaction isn't one of popcorn, a hot-looking date, and a bright Saturday afternoon at the local matinee.

My first reaction was the scene in *Casino Royale*, where James Bond is tied naked to a chair and tortured by the villain Le Chiffre with a long swinging rope knotted at the end with a hard loop the size of a grapefruit. But I tried not to dwell too much on such unpleasant images. I was already scared enough.

And still hoping I'd wake up in my bedroom.

But at least I wasn't naked.

"Here's what we're gonna do. I ask you a question. You don't give me the right answer, I pick a great scene from a movie, and we go from there. Sound okay?"

"I guess it depends on which great scene you're going to pick, doesn't it?"

"I've got some great scenes already picked out."

"I can only imagine what they are."

"You'll know what they are if I don't get the answers I want."

"I sort of figured that one out."

"Good. We're on the same page. Now. Ready for the first question?"

"No, but I have the distinct feeling you're going to ask anyway."

"For an idiot, you're pretty damn bright."

"Thank you. They say intelligence runs in my family."

"Why the disguise?"

"Is that the first question?"

"You really *are* bright."

I figured honesty would be the best policy--at least in *this* instance. "I didn't want anyone to know it was me."

He sighed and picked up the hammer.

My cell beeped.

He put the hammer down. "Yours?"

"I believe so."

It beeped again.

His eyes focused on my hip pocket. He seemed to be waiting for me to do something.

"I'd *love* to answer that, but these irritating zip-ties make moving my arms a tad difficult."

He bent over, pulled it out and checked the display. "Says . . . Mom . . ."

Great. Mom and her perfect timing. But in this case I was actually relieved.

I shrugged. "My mother. What can I say?"

"Important?"

"If I don't answer, she'll worry. And she hasn't been well."

"Sick?"

"She puts up a brave front, but we all know she's slipping fast." Mom was in great shape for sixty-four, but I suspected Mr. Hood wouldn't be nearly as sympathetic if he knew my mother still looked damned good in a swimsuit.

He sighed. "Guess I'd better let you talk to her, then."

He certainly was agreeable for a sadist. He no doubt had mother issues as well.

"Watch yourself, all right?"

I nodded. Any distraction was better than watching my brains slide down the front of my Hawaiian shirt once that damned hammer started swinging. "It should only take a sec."

He flicked it on and stuck it close to my ear. He slid his chair closer. "Just don't say anything stupid."

"I hope you realize how hard that will be for me."

He held up his fist in warning. It was almost as big as the one the doorman used to take my camera.

"Hi, Mom."

"Ralphie, I was just talking to your uncle a few minutes ago--"

"Which one?"

"Nicky, of course."

"How *is* Uncle Nicky?"

"Doing as well as expected. His arthritis is bothering him, as usual. But when you're almost seventy, you expect things like that."

Uncle Nicky's arthritis was bothering him when I was in grade school. But he was a favorite uncle, and anyway this wasn't the time to quibble about the man's physical condition. I was much too concerned about *my* physical condition at the moment.

"Why the call, Mom?"

"We both want you to come down here and spend the weekend. Nicky has a couple of projects he'd like you to help him with, and since he can't handle much himself anymore--"

"Mom? Now is *not* a good time for this."

"You *never* have time for your mother anymore."

"I'm just a little busy right now."

"Ralphie, what are you doing that's so important?"

"I'm about to be--"

Mr. Hood nudged me.

138

"She asked." I shrugged. "You can't lie to your mother. They always know."

"Ralphie? What're you doing?"

"I'm about to get hurt. And please don't call me Ralphie."

Silence.

"What are you talking about?"

"I'm with this guy, and we're playing a game--
"

"*Watch* it . . ." The fist moved closer.

"I wish you'd be serious once in a while."

"Believe me, if you saw me right now, you'd know I was being as serious as heart failure."

A pause. "You're really playing a *game*? With a *man*?"

"Yep."

"This game . . . what is it?"

"We haven't started yet."

"Who *is* this person you're playing with?"

"He hasn't introduced himself."

"Is he one of those . . . *nasties* you're always going after?"

"I'd say that would be a good guess."

"Have you seen him before?"

"I don't know. He's wearing a hood."

"You're *kidding*."

"Why would I kid about something like *that*?"

"A real *hood*? Like those country people wear in Mississippi?"

"This one's black."

"He's a *black* man?"

"His hood is black."

"He's . . . not wearing a *sheet*, is he?"

"A sweatshirt and sweatpants."

"What's she talking about?" Mr. Hood whispered.

"She wants to know what you're wearing."

"Why?"

"She's worried you're with the Klan."

He sighed.

"Ask him who he is," Mom said.

"I don't think he'll tell me."

"Tell you what?" he asked.

"Who you are."

He shook his head.

"I didn't think so."

"Let me talk to him," Mom said.

"My mother wants to talk to you."

His eyes blinked inside the hood.

"Would I *lie* about that?"

He grabbed the phone and put it to his ear. "Yeah?" A moment later: "I can't tell you that, ma'am." Another pause. "Yes, ma'am." Silence. "No, ma'am." He sighed. "I understand. Yes, ma'am. No problem."

He shoved the cell back into my pocket.

"What did she say?"

"She told me to be careful and make sure you don't get hurt."

"Sounds like something she'd say."

"She also said I should make sure you're eating the right foods. And you're to come down to Lauderdale as soon as you can." He picked up the hammer. "Now. Where were we?"

"I can't remember."

"Nice try but guess what."

"*You* remember?"

"Bingo."

"Then why ask?"

He shrugged a massive shoulder. "I figured I'd be nice. For your mom's sake. She sounds okay."

"She'd like that. She'd also like it if you just put the hammer away. It would be a terrific ice-breaker."

He kept it in his hands.

I didn't think that would work. But it sure was worth a try.

"As I said before: Why the disguise?"

"And as *I* said, I didn't want anyone to know it was me. You know how the *paparazzi* are if they think you're a celebrity. I duck into a public toilet for a few minutes of quiet time and the next thing I know, six sweaty guys with cameras are hanging over the top of the stall, ready to snap the grand event before I even have time to flush."

"You're clever but guess what."

"You didn't like my answer?"

"Good guess. Now we come to the movie part. The first movie we're gonna play is *Payback*. Ever heard of it?"

"*Payback, Payback . . .*" I knew what he was getting at. I also knew what the hammer was for. But instead of fainting or wetting my pants, I decided to act stupid. You can avoid a lot of unnecessary aggravation by acting stupid. I'd done

141

it all my life and it worked better than anything else. Besides, being clever just wasn't working with his dude. "I'm not sure. Who was in it?"

"Mel Gibson."

"Is he that short Jewish guy who starred in *Spaceballs*? Ever hear of it? John Candy and Rick Moranis? Wasn't that Dark Helmet guy funny? I also liked it when--"

"Listen to me, asshole. We both know you're being a dumbass again, so I'll spell it out for you. Mel Gibson was where you're at now, and the bad guy was where I'm at. Guess what happens now."

"My guess is that Mr. Hammer is about to upstage both of us."

"You *are* bright for a dumbass." He raised the hammer.

I gritted my teeth, forced my eyes shut, held my breath . . .

"Now you've *really* gotten yourself into a pickle," the brunette said.

My eyes shot open.

She was standing directly behind Mr. Hood, wearing denim shorts and a red halter top. Her hair hung loose. Her hands rested on her hips.

"How the hell did you--"

"What?" Mr. Hood said. His hammer, raised at a level just above his head, stopped abruptly. "You got something to say?"

"Tell him," the brunette said.

Mr. Hood continued staring at me. She was standing there right behind him and had just said something, but he hadn't heard her. He was staring at *me*.

Oh my God. I'd been right all along. She *wasn't* real.

"You're . . . *not* real," I whispered.

"You really *are* a good detective," she said.

"What the hell are you trying to do *now*, asshole?" Mr. Hood asked.

"Tell him," she said.

"He won't believe me."

"Try him."

He turned around in his seat and looked right at her, then turned back to me. "Who the *fuck* do you think you're--"

"There's a gorgeous brunette standing there," I said. "Right behind you. She's about five-six, one-ten--"

"Actually, I weighed one-twelve in my peak," she said.

"Sorry. One-twelve."

"You're funny," Mr. Hood said. "*Real* funny."

"You *honestly* think I'm gorgeous?" she asked.

"No one ever said that before?"

"Maybe you're just really glad to see me."

"You can say *that* again."

"Yeah," Mr. Hood said, nodding. "One real funny smartass who's gonna be hobbling around on nine toes in about five seconds."

"You want me to get you out of this?" she asked.

"Yes. Please. That is, if you're not too busy right now."

143

"Smartass," Mr. Hood said. "I ain't busy at all. I got more than enough time to have some fun with those toes."

"I'm not busy at the moment," my hallucination said. She stared at Mr. Hood, then blinked.

A cell phone buzzed.

This time it wasn't mine.

"God*dammi*t. . . ." The hammer dropped loudly on the floor. Mr. Hood groaned and dug into his pocket. "You're lucky. *Real* lucky. After *Payback* we were gonna move on to *Lethal Weapon*. Heard of *that* one?"

"There were four of those, weren't there?"

"The first one's the one you should worry about. Remember the deal with the jumper cables and the wet sponge?"

"Can't say that I do."

He pointed to the jumper cables dangling from his metal rack. Then flipped open the cell, turned and walked away.

"That was *you*?" I asked the brunette.

She shrugged.

"How'd you *do* that?"

She smiled. "It's really nothing."

Mr. Hood began yelling. "Hello, dammit! Who the fuck's on the line?" He checked his voicemail, sighed, then flipped the cell shut and came back. "I'll be right back. Don't go nowhere, okay?"

"You wouldn't by any chance have a magazine I could look at while you're gone, would you? Maybe an old *Penthouse*?"

144

"You really *are* funny for a dumbass." He rushed past me. A metal door slammed shut somewhere behind me.

I eyed the tool rack six feet in front of me.

The machete hanging from it seemed my best bet.

"You wouldn't by any chance want to bring that machete over here, would you?"

"I would if I could . . ." She shrugged.

"I understand."

"Good. But if I were you, I'd hurry. I don't know how long you have before he finds out no one called him. When he comes back, he'll probably be upset."

I dragged the chair toward the metal rack.

She'd already vanished.

Chapter 17

The warehouse stood in a small grassy field about two hundred feet directly behind Vesper's, at the far end of the paved lot used for employees and deliveries.

In my haste to leave I didn't take time to investigate. But I could easily tell that the building was used for other purposes. Palettes of slot machines and gaming tables filled various cubicles. Lockers marked *Maintenance* and *Cleaning Supplies* covered an entire wall. Several stalls allotted to house the big bosses' expensive rides faced the garage doors. Sealed-off sections toward the back, secured with chains and padlocks, drew my suspicion.

By the time I freed myself with the blade of the machete and went back out into the glaring Florida sunshine, Vesper's was packed. A sloppy-dressed tourist clumsily inching his way down the gravel lot in his bare feet wouldn't cause much concern. Florida seems to encourage all sorts of strange people walking around. Besides, the doormen were too busy taking money from the growing crowd at the entrance to care what was going on somewhere else.

I'd have no trouble returning to the rented Nissan.

"Hey, man!"

One row down, a tall, skinny guy in a black leather vest, jeans and black leather boots leaned against an old Firebird. He was around twenty-five and covered with tattoos. He smoked a cigarette and watched me the same way you'd stare at a strange tropical fish in an aquarium.

His ride looked like an early seventies model. The paint job, faded and peeling, couldn't disguise the beauty of the powerful machine beneath it. I loved my TransAm but wouldn't mind owning a classic like that.

"Hey to you, too," I said casually.

He pointed to the ground at my feet. "You're in your bare feet."

"Really?" I glanced down. "I was wondering why the ground felt so rough and hot."

"That's 'cause you're in your bare feet."

"You're right. Thanks."

His eyes were glazed. His cigarette appeared home-made. "You do that a lot?"

"Do what a lot?"

"Walk around in your bare feet much?"

"Only when I leave my apartment without my shoes."

He gave that some thought, sucking in smoke, holding it in for a few seconds, then pushing out the thick gray cloud. He coughed, then cleared his throat. "Better put on some shoes. You can really fuck up your feet that way."

"Thanks. I'll tend to that right now."

"Shoes are important, man."

"Don't I know it." I loved people who cared about one another. You just didn't see enough genuine charity and love these days.

147

"You fuck up your feet? That's it."

"I'll remember that." Something occurred to me. "What are you doing here? You the parking lot attendant?"

"Came to see my woman, works in there. She's a dancer. Good one, too."

"I'll bet."

"Gorillas at the door don't like my threads. Told me to get lost."

"Some people."

"Assholes, man."

"World's full of them."

"You got *that* right." He got in his ride, fired it up and eased out of his spot.

The Nissan, thank God, hadn't budged. I'd left my wallet under the back seat, wedged beneath the small plastic emergency toolkit provided by the rental agency. Judging from the number of vehicles in the lot, my enemies didn't have the time to send anyone to look for my ride.

My keys still rested on the inside bottom lip of the rear bumper. I'd read somewhere that a smart private eye will leave them there or on the axle if he suspects he's about to be kidnapped or robbed.

Mr. Hood probably left my cell phone alone because they didn't care or just didn't want to spend time going through my voicemail.

I returned to the car rental on Semoran Boulevard at around six, picked up the TransAm from their back lot and was on my way back to my apartment by six-thirty.

My cell phone went off as I turned onto Curry Ford Road.

It was Neil Haversack.

"What's up?" I asked.

"I was gonna ask you the same thing."

"I'm on my way home from Vesper's."

"So what were you doing there?" Neil asked. "I didn't think you had the money for lap dances."

"Playing a game with one of their goons."

"You were *what*?"

"Ever see the movie, *Payback*?"

"Years ago."

"Remember the scene with the ball-peen hammer?"

"They emulsified a couple of Mel Gibson's toes. Good scene."

"Someone knocked me out and took me to their warehouse."

"What's this have to do with *Payback*?"

"One of their goons tried playing that same game with my toes."

Neil sighed. "How bad were you hurt this time?"

"Not bad at all. The goon with the hammer got a sudden phone call and had to politely excuse himself."

Another sigh. "I'm telling you, Deacon, you've had more good luck lately than ten guys. I take it you didn't find out anything about your deadbeat dad."

"I think I might have pissed off someone close to him. What do *you* think?"

149

"Like I told you before, you're in *way* over your head."

"I can't let a little thing like that stop me, can I?"

"You want my advice?"

"Not really."

"Good. Here it is. You're small-time. You go after petty thieves, deadbeats and bail jumpers. This is a *crime family* we're talking about and some of them are on the city's payroll. They want their privacy and don't mind paying big bucks to drop off a minor irritation into the ocean. Someone like you doesn't stand a chance."

"I can't very well quit, can I? I'll get a reputation."

"For what?"

"Quitting."

"You might end up losing more than your rep if you're not careful."

"I'll be careful."

"You never have been before."

"It's never too late to try something new."

I stopped at the light at the intersection of Conway and Curry Ford.

I started thinking about my hallucination again. Wondering who she was and why she looked so familiar.

Now that I knew she was dead, it put a whole new perspective on the situation.

I still found it difficult to believe. I also found it difficult to figure out why it was happening in the first place.

But as important as that was, it didn't seem to matter. The important thing was that it was *indeed* happening. She popped up as a real person and no one saw her but me. She spoke real words that no one heard but me.

I rubbed my eyes. This was making me tired. Whatever they'd used to knock me out had given me a splitting headache. I needed to get home, take some aspirin, have a drink and lie down. Then I could think about things a little better.

When my vision cleared, the brunette was sitting beside me in the same outfit she wore in the warehouse.

"Damn. You pop up at the strangest times."

"Are you complaining?"

"Hell, no. But you're gonna have to tell me how you do all that."

"All what?"

"The popping-up thing."

"One day, maybe."

"And the purpose for this visit?"

"Don't go home."

"Want to tell me why?"

"Some really nasty people are waiting for you there."

Interesting. Yesterday they'd just left without a word or a calling card. This time they'd decided to stay and wait for me. It sure hadn't taken them long at all to find out where I lived.

But why would they go through all this? Was it because I was getting too close to something they didn't want me to know about? My professional instinct told me this involved something more than just one deadbeat dad.

"Are these the same gents who wanted to turn my toes into roast beef?"

"You know they are."

I eased through the intersection when the light changed. "They need anger management," I said. "Maybe we can discuss that when I get home."

"You don't scare off, do you?"

"Not when someone's already paid me. You get scared away, the word gets out, you're labeled a wimp and the jobs quit coming. You can't pay your rent, get kicked out of your office and have to get a boring office job, or roasting weenies at the local mall. It's a vicious cycle."

"That guy wearing the hood was right."

"How?"

"He said you were funny."

"I thought you already knew that."

"I did. But do me a favor?"

"Sure."

"Be careful." Then she vanished.

I went down the block, pulled into the 7-Eleven and called Neil.

"Now what?"

"There seems to be some sort of illegal party going on in the neighborhood."

"What neighborhood?"

"My place on South Conway."

"The same people you've been pissing off?"

"They're waiting for me. I don't know how many there are."

"They're at *your* place?"

"Apparently."

"How do you know?"

"Don't ask."

"You talking breaking and entering?"

"I don't remember giving them my key."

"Where are you now?"

"At a 7-Eleven one block south."

"Wait there. And don't do anything stupid."

"What do you want me to do first?"

"You're *such* a dickhead."

"It's a God-given talent."

"Just keep it in check for a little while."

"How long?"

"As long as it takes us to get there."

"But I'm obviously the guest of honor."

"Deacon . . ."

"I know, I know. Stop being a dickhead."

"Here's what I want you to do. Wait there, don't do anything stupid and put your dickhead meter on hold. And give us fifteen minutes."

"Hope I can remember all that."

"Play with yourself or something."

"You don't have to be insulting."

"Sure I do. I'm a cop--remember?"

***

Neil and three other cops showed up in a black-and-white and an unmarked car.

They parked on the other side of the pool in the center of the complex behind the privacy fence, where they couldn't be seen from my apartment.

153

I parked in my usual space and sat there, staring at my living room window, which was dark and still, except for the occasional fluttering of the drapes caused by the air-conditioning duct in the floor.

I was obviously dealing with pros. Only pros had the resources to quickly find out who you were and where you lived. And pros usually meant mob. When the mob was involved, it used its resources. They could afford the best help. Anyone could break into someone's place, but it took a high-priced pro to break in without leaving a trail.

I was reasonably certain that whoever had paid me a visit the day before left the door ajar to scare me into backing off. It had nothing to do with forgetting to close it.

Pros didn't forget anything.

My cell buzzed.

It was Neil. "You going in or what?"

"Just gathering the courage."

"We can go in with you."

"I think I should do this myself."

"It might get rough if you go in alone."

"They won't try anything if you go in with me."

"You *want* them to try something?"

"I want you to nail them for something more than just breaking and entering."

"You sure can be stubborn sometimes, Deacon. I just hope your good luck streak holds out."

"You and me both."

"All right, then . . . We'll wait thirty seconds, then go in fast. Just make sure your door's unlocked."

"Thirty seconds?" That sounded like a long time.

"You want to have a *drink* with them first?"

I didn't want to sound like a wimp so I said, "That's fine," all the while knowing a lot could happen in thirty seconds.

"Let's rock," Neil said.

I got out of the TransAm, went up the walk and unlocked the door.

As soon as the door opened, my professional nose detected the faintest scent of cheap cologne. I took a deep breath and flicked on the living room light.

Two goons sitting on my living room couch stared indifferently at me. They were around forty, had shaved heads and wore dark suits. They looked like church ushers, but with a blank expression instead of the usual look of irritation I remembered on the ushers I knew as a child.

"Comfortable?" I said.

They both stood. They weren't as large as the doormen at Vesper's, but not much smaller. And they appeared more than capable--especially when both reached into their pockets at the same time.

I wondered how much of those thirty seconds had already elapsed.

Knowing I should be away from the door when Neil and his guys stormed in, I took two steps toward the dining room area. By that time, both of my visitors had produced brass knuckles and held them in strike position. One moved right toward me while his companion circled in the opposite direction, separating me from the door.

"Aren't those illegal?"

Neither replied.

They *were* pros. Pros hardly spoke at all.

"You actually *need* those? You each outweigh me by fifty pounds."

The first one shrugged.

The other just looked bored.

"You two weren't here yesterday afternoon by any chance, were you?"

They both shrugged.

"Has it been thirty seconds yet?"

The first one said, "Huh?"

"Since I came in."

They both stared at one another.

"I'm expecting company."

"Company?" the first one asked.

"Good memory."

The door burst open.

Neil and his buddies rushed in, guns drawn and ready.

"*Police! Freeze!*"

The goons stopped moving and quickly raised their arms. Both sets of brass knuckles thumped quietly to the carpet.

I hurried the last few feet to the kitchen counter and grabbed my trusty bottle of Jack's. My hands shook as I poured my drink.

Chapter 18

Early the next morning, just as I was finishing breakfast, I got a call from someone with a soft voice who said his name was Tony Simon.

I knew enough about hoods to suspect the name was probably a shortened form of Anthony Simonetti, or maybe even Antonio de Salmonella. Italians often Americanized their names to blend in or appear less mob-like. Some had nose-jobs and dyed their hair. The intelligent ones even went to college to learn business, financing and how to speak correctly without sounding like a Neanderthal.

"Am I speaking to Mister Deacon?"

"Guilty on both counts." His New York accent was faint. He probably attended one of those fancy colleges. I'd been in Florida long enough to recognize most accents. I knew when I was speaking to a Snow Bird, a recent transplant or just some guy in town for a few days who wanted to do the theme-park thing with his family.

Latin accents, on the other hand, are nearly impossible to pin down. I know Latins who've been here since they were two and even after thirty years living in Florida, they still sound like they'd just come up with the latest flotilla.

Simon was quite possibly some sort of legal mob representative. Since I was apparently causing problems for Vesper's and since the Raguzzo's owned Vesper's, Simon probably worked for them. And since I'd embarrassed some important people the night before, Simon was probably ordered to straighten this out. In mob language, that meant doing whatever it took to make this go away. It didn't take much to embarrass rich, powerful Italians. They were so hung-up about honor and respect that it twisted their perception of things. Crime families valued their privacy and hated answering questions. They didn't like it one bit that I'd managed to get away from them more than once after trying to ask questions or that I'd had two of their men arrested the night before. Outwitting three of them in my office the day before had also put their panties in a twist.

Most of all, my still being alive probably really bugged them.

But I had to remind myself that with the Raguzzo's--as well as any other successful crime family--this was just business. There was nothing personal about hitting me over the head . . . or punching me in the gut . . . or zip-tying me to a chair and threatening my unprotected toes with a ball-peen hammer. That was just how they handled things.

"Why are you calling?" I asked Simon.

"I would like to meet with you on behalf of my employer to discuss some very important matters."

"Your employer?"

"Correct."

"You don't work for a pest control company, do you? My apartment complex has an exclusive contract with--"

"No, Mr. Deacon." His voice sounded like it held the hint of a smile. A laugh was out of the question. Legal representatives wouldn't permit themselves the luxury of a laugh. Very few lawyers I knew actually laughed. They usually forced out a kind of awkward smile that made them look like they were passing gas or a tiny gall stone. "Not exactly a *pest* control company . . ."

I didn't like the way he'd emphasized the word *pest*. It indicated that the word *control* went right along with *company*. "Care to tell me who your employer is?"

"I am not permitted to discuss him specifically."

"Just a little-bitty hint?"

"He doesn't wish his name mentioned when discussing business matters."

"If I guess, would you tell me?"

His silence told me my answer.

"Does this call have anything to do with those gentlemen I found in my apartment last night?"

"Among other things . . ."

"I didn't want them there, you know."

"We assumed you didn't."

"It wasn't personal. I just didn't invite them."

"Of course not."

"They're not exactly in my social sphere."

"I understand."

"I prefer my friends more animated and less likely to set off metal detectors."

"I can see why you didn't approve."

159

"They were sprawled on my living room couch when I came in."

"That was extremely *gauche*."

"There was a heel print on my coffee table."

"I must apologize for that. Was there any damage to your furniture?"

"A scuff mark. A little Pledge and some elbow grease took care of it."

"I am sorry for the inconvenience."

"I had no choice but to send them away in a squad car."

"I understand."

"Luckily, my cop buddies were with me. They like to come see me from time to time."

"Very fortunate for you, wasn't it?"

"Otherwise, I might have lost my temper and done something I'd probably regret later on."

"I sympathize."

Apparently Simon didn't care much about the two goons. He was most likely the prissy type who didn't like getting his hands dirty.

"I sure am glad for their sakes that they were able to get safely away with their police escorts," I added.

"My sentiments exactly. Now . . . if we could just make some arrangements to meet . . ."

"Any suggestions?"

"You pick the place."

"Why me? You're the one asking me out."

"I'd like to show you I'm sincere."

"Oh, I know you're sincere."

"How would you? We've never met before."

160

"I'm sure you work for only the sincerest of individuals, right?"

"Correct."

"And you're letting me pick the rendezvous spot to make me think I'm in full control of the situation and that no hanky-panky will come of it?"

"If you select the location, you'll feel safer and won't be tempted to keep looking over your shoulder. This way, we can concentrate on our talk."

"What's to prevent you from being followed by half a dozen armed men on the way over to meet me?"

"*Paisano* . . . I'm doing my best to arrange a nice, quiet meeting. Just the two of us enjoying a cup of cappuccino, a little soft music--"

"Sounds suspiciously romantic. You're not funny, are you?"

"Funny?"

"You know. Not a manly man."

"There is no need to worry about *that*, my friend."

"I usually share my cappuccino and soft music with a chick. You know. Long hair? Lots and lots of delicious curves? Smells good? Soft all over?"

He cleared his throat. "So . . . how about a place for our little talk?"

"There's a great restaurant in town, one block down from OPD--"

"Now why should we meet in town? All that traffic. Those horrible exhaust fumes.

161

Inconsiderate people bumping into you. All sorts of loud, bothersome noises."

"That's right. What was I thinking?"

"Pick a nice place. A popular local eatery will be preferable. Perhaps one the tourists love. This way, you'll feel safe in a crowd of people."

"Tourist places are out."

"Why is that?"

"The ones that serve tourists should be closed down. They offer the type of crap you'd expect in a Mexican jail."

"Disgusting. Why do the tourists put up with it?"

"They're only here a few days. The restaurants toss food at them, rush them out and get ready for the next batch. Like feeding chickens, only more time-consuming and much messier."

"I'm glad you told me. So where does this leave us?"

"How about the Florida Mall? They have an eatery that's not bad. Not even for a mall."

"What is the name?"

"Kenny's. It's always crowded and nearly surrounded with window booths. I'll be able to see anyone coming close to the place."

"Sounds good. Name a time."

I was about twenty minutes away from the area. It would take Simon a few minutes to get his details organized with his people. If he was going to set me up, it might take him ten or fifteen minutes to arrange it--unless, of course, he'd already done it. But since I was pretty sure he wasn't local, he wasn't familiar with the area. It would take him a little time to find it. The eatery was sandwiched between a lingerie shop and a computer store and didn't open until ten.

This gave me time to think of several courses of action.

I told Simon, "Ten o'clock." Then I hung up, finished my breakfast, grabbed my gun and rushed out of the apartment.

Chapter 19

Florida Mall's enormous parking lot was about one-quarter filled.

I waited in the TransAm in the shade of one of the few trees left standing, about twenty spaces down from the Sand Lake turnoff. From my vantage point I watched the heavy traffic roaring down both Sand Lake Road and Orange Blossom Trail.

The south side of the Mall remained hidden to me. I'd have to make periodic rounds to properly scope the entire building. Such a trip would probably take ten minutes or longer, dodging Mall traffic and shoppers. But since I didn't want to give up my parking space, I didn't bother. Mostly everyone used the Sand Lake entrance. Nearly all the traffic coming in from the Trail circled the big complex anyway. Checking that end seemed pointless.

I wore my Pittsburgh Pirates baseball cap that Uncle Nicky bought me when I was in high school. I also wore my wraparounds, a loose-fitting dark-blue tee shirt, faded jeans and tennis shoes. The Beretta, comfortably hidden beneath the baggy tee shirt, sat in a pancake holster wedged in the small of my back.

I looked no different from the other tourists wandering around. Tony Simon would have no way of knowing what I looked like. I was comfortable in my anonymity.

Everyone passing the TransAm made me wonder if my hallucination was close. I hoped so. I felt much safer with her looking out for me. I knew it was stupid and seriously mental to depend on a hallucination to get you out of jams, but I couldn't help it. When someone keeps saving your life, it puts things in a different perspective. Besides, she'd been right about everything so far and I trusted her. Clint Eastwood once said that a wise man knew his limitations. I'd always been aware of mine but never let them get in the way of my determination.

Which is probably why I got beat up so much.

My cell went off. It was my mother.

"Ralphie, are you all right?"

"Mom, I'm busy right now. And please don't call me Ralphie."

"I've been worried about you all night. That person I talked to--"

"He said you sounded nice."

A pause. "Is he the one who was playing that game with you?"

"Yes, Mom."

Another pause. "And he said I was . . . *nice*?"

"You got it."

"Ralphie, you know it's not nice to try and fool your mother."

"Now why would I want to do something like that? And don't call me Ralphie."

"You've been doing it since you were five. I think you like it."

"Listen, Mom, I'm okay, all right? And I've got things to do."

"Did he . . . hurt you?"

"Not really."

"Why do I think he did?"

"You're that way, Mom. Always the worrier. Always thinking something bad's gonna happen."

"Something bad usually does."

"That's beside the point."

"What were you two doing? I mean really?"

"Business, Mom."

"Then why'd you tell me about that game?"

"I couldn't think of anything else to say."

"That wasn't very nice. I was up half the night, worrying. He sounded dangerous. Shifty-eyed."

Shifty-eyed? How could she tell? But I knew better than ask.

"You know I can take care of myself."

"I don't know anything of the sort. The only time you ever made a really intelligent decision was when you married Felicia. Then you two divorced and put me through all kinds of hell all over again."

My mother could make a mosquito feel guilty for stinging her. I didn't know if it was the Italian in her, the Catholic upbringing, the mother instinct or a combination of all three. But she was an expert at it. Even though I was forty, she could load me up with the same guilt she used when I occasionally skipped Catechism class with the other guys to sneak down to the creek behind the church and catch tadpoles.

166

"Sorry, Mom. We didn't mean to put you through all kinds of hell."

"Do you see her at all nowadays?"

"Once in a while."

"How's she doing?"

"All right, I guess." I didn't want her to know Phil was doing infinitely better than when we were married. That would've kept my mother on the line another half-hour.

"Any chance you two might--"

"I don't think so."

"You're sure?"

"Positive."

She sighed. "Tell her I said hi, then."

"I will."

"And stop lying to me. It keeps me awake nights."

"I will."

"And start thinking about coming down here. Uncle Nicky has that project he wants you to help him with."

"I will."

"And take care of yourself."

"I will."

"And stop hanging around with people like that . . . that character I talked to. I don't know what you two were doing, but he just didn't sound right. I don't think he was brought up very well."

Sometimes my mother's intuition was frightening. "How'd you get *that*?"

"A feeling I had. He sounded . . . not quite right."

"And shifty-eyed."

"That, too."

"You're really good, Mom."

"It's taken you all these years to find that out?"

"I knew it in grade school. I just didn't want to tell you."

"Why not?"

"You'd get an attitude."

"What kind of attitude?"

"The kind you have now, only worse."

"Oh, stop."

"I will."

"And start eating better foods. Want me to send you some ravioli or lasagna? It would be much better if you came down here and ate it with us. Then you and your uncle could work on that tool shed he'd like to build behind his patio. It would be a nice visit."

"I'll be down soon."

"Don't lie, now."

"I won't."

"You promise?"

"Yes, Mom."

"In the meantime, promise me you'll start eating better."

"I will."

At 10:05, I got out of the TransAm. I decided it would be safer to blend in until I was safely inside the building.

Staggered groups of tourists and customers strolled casually down the wide aisles. I got behind two middle-aged women discussing some man they

168

both knew. Judging from their conversation, he was their boss and was doing both of them. They both knew it but he didn't know they knew, and they were planning something interesting for him.

They were both attractive, but I knew how nasty women could get when they found out they were being used. I didn't envy him.

The Mall was doing its usual late-morning business. Everyone wandered around, looking lost, spaced-out, or just downright bored. The majority flocked the fast-food mall. Most shoppers stared blankly at the store window displays. Kids ran around like monkeys freed from their cages. I was tempted to trip one or two but managed to keep my cool.

Kenny's was packed. I set about looking for a table, but they were all taken. Toward the rear, a good-looking dark-haired guy in a charcoal-gray suit stood up and waved. He looked like he could be an undertaker or a wise guy straight out of *Goodfellas*. I was surprised that he'd beaten me here. He probably got here while I was talking to my mother.

I also didn't like it that he could pick me out of the crowd so easily.

My hallucination did say they knew what I looked like, didn't she?

I scanned the premises as I went down the aisle, my senses alert for quick movements, such as a gun or a steak knife coming into view. Most of the customers were women, older couples and teens that should have been in school.

Everyone looked dangerous, but that was just my paranoia doing its job.

I also kept an eye out for my hallucination. I didn't know what she'd do in a crowded restaurant. It would be embarrassing to see her sitting in a booth with other people. I wouldn't know if I should strike up a conversation or just ignore her. I just hoped she wouldn't put me in that position. She'd already embarrassed me at Smilin' Susie's.

Luckily, I didn't think she was anywhere in the room.

Up close, Tony Simon resembled an undertaker. His skin had that same sort of death-parlor pallor. His coal-black hair was combed straight back--not one hair out of place. His cheeks were clean-shaven--not a hint of stubble. His large, clear black eyes stayed on me. His manicured nails glimmered in the lighting. His impeccably pressed silk suit suggested it was incapable of developing a wrinkle or tolerating a piece of lint.

"Mr. Deacon?"

"Yes . . ."

"I'm Tony Simon." He was an inch taller than me. That also bothered me. I never could trust anyone taller than me.

"How'd you know it was me?"

He shrugged. "You have the air of a man who is definitely looking for someone."

"I was."

"And now you've found me."

His statement made me feel trapped in some weird French flick about *déjà vu*. Or a prison movie where the main character is released so he can hook up with the mobster who'd sprung him. I thought of Humphrey Bogart and Jimmy Cagney and wondered if Barton MacLane was waiting to pounce on me somewhere else later on.

His handshake was warm and brief. "Please. Sit."

I sat and put my wraparounds on the table. He joined me, held up an arm and clicked his fingers. I guessed he assumed this was a ritzy place, where the clicking of fingers instantly earned the attention of some tall, skinny guy in a monkey suit named Garson. Here, no one seemed to care. Everyone was busy gulping food, gabbing or both. I could tell right then that he wasn't local. If you expected instant service and professionalism in Florida, you were obviously from somewhere else.

He probably expected the food to be excellent, too. Florida was known for many things, but instant service and professionalism weren't among them. Neither was excellent food.

A slight, middle-aged female wearing a bouffant hairdo, too much makeup and a permanent scowl took her time coming over. Her nametag said *Hi! I'm RUTH*. "Coffee?" she asked in a bored voice.

"I'll have a Cappuccino," Tony Simon said.

"Plain coffee for me," I said.

"*Plain* coffee?" Simon's pinched expression suggested I'd just ordered dog turds on stale bread.

"Nothing's wrong with *your* hearing, is there?"

"But I'm buying . . ." It sounded like the explanation to end all explanations. He obviously wanted me to order something special.

Ruth stood there, skinny arms crossed, growing more bored by the second.

I'd always been leery of people who insisted on paying the tab--especially people who didn't know me.

"I'd like it very much if you ordered whatever you wish."

"Really? I can order *anything*?"

He nodded eagerly. "Yes. Please."

"Good. I'd like plain coffee."

He sighed. "Whatever you wish . . ."

I turned to the waitress. "Ruthie? Plain coffee, please."

She hurried away.

"So you're the man causing all this trouble for my bosses." Simon had apparently recovered from the coffee-ordering incident. His pleasant smile showed perfect white teeth. I was hoping to see at least *one* imperfection. Seeing none made me distrust him even more. Bad enough I was forced to see perfect people every time I switched on the TV. I didn't want to see any in real-life.

"That's me," I said proudly. "A natural-born troublemaker."

"Obviously."

"I don't look it, do I?"

"Actually, you look just like all these other tourists."

172

"I like blending in. It's healthier that way. See, I tend to occasionally meet people who pay other people to hurt guys like me."

Ruth brought our coffees, set them on the table and turned to leave.

"We'll be ready to order in a few minutes," Simon said.

Her permanent scowl deepening, she walked away without a word. She wouldn't be easy to woo. Not even for a good-looking, soft-spoken Italian in designer threads and an impressive expense account.

I put sugar in my coffee, stirred and tasted it. It scalded my tongue. I blew on it, had another swallow and scalded it a second time. Practice makes perfect.

"Tell me something," I said.

"Certainly."

"Why are we here?"

His understated smile was amiable and probably socially correct. "You get to the point, don't you?"

"I don't like to waste time. If you were a luscious blond babe, I'd be gazing into your eyes, wondering what you're wearing underneath your outfit. I'd spend a lot of time fantasizing about what we'd be doing later on."

"I see."

"But you're not a luscious blonde and you're definitely not female."

"No . . ."

"So start talking. I've got things to do, people to annoy."

"You *are* a character, Mr. Deacon."

"*Such* perception."

"I've been told you're partly Italian. I can see it in your hair color, your eyes. But your features-- they're obviously *not* Italian."

"Thank you."

Simon kept his pleasant smile. "That wasn't meant to be a compliment *or* insult."

"My father was Scotch-Irish, with some German tossed in there somewhere." I was curious how they knew so much about me. As Neil said, they had people in high places. You never really notice this until someone you never met before tells you about your relatives.

"So your mother was Italian?"

"Still is."

"She's still alive, I take it?"

"You're good."

"What part of the old country is she from?"

"A very old section of Pittsburgh. The South Hills. The Clairton area."

"Her *family*, I meant."

"The ankle."

"Where, exactly?"

"Calabria. San Mango."

He nodded knowingly.

"Ever been there?"

"I've heard of it." Simon sipped his Cappuccino. "My employer would like to make you an offer."

"Don't tell me *he's* a luscious blonde."

"I'm sorry, but you're wrong on both counts."

174

"I was hoping I might get lucky."

"You just might."

"He's got a luscious blond sister? Daughter?"

"Have you ever given any thought to branching out in your profession?"

"How?"

"Working for a much larger organization."

"Don't tell me Old Man Raguzzo's actually offering me a *job*."

He said nothing.

I wanted to laugh. I'd obviously embarrassed them more than I thought.

"What kind of offer are we talking about?"

"A sort of administrative position."

That sounded like a fancy way of saying they wanted to bury me in an office somewhere. Probably in Alaska. Or maybe Timbuktu.

"Doing what?"

"It would be easy, highly-paid work. Screening out prospective clients visiting the plant."

"Plant?"

"One of my employer's many interests is plastics. Computer plastics. He owns plants in Orlando, Lake Mary, Tampa--"

"And where would this position be?"

"Wherever you're needed."

"Is there one in Alaska?"

"I'm not sure. I'm certain he'd consider your choice of placement."

"How about Honolulu?"

"I don't believe he owns a plant there, but if you'd like to relocate to Hawaii, I'm sure there could be some sort of arrangement made that would benefit--"

"Can you read my forehead?"

"Pardon?"

The bill of my baseball cap was pulled down too much. Mindful of my goose egg, I pushed the bill up. "Now can you see it?"

"Yes . . ."

"See the word *stupid* written there?"

"Mr. Deacon, I assure you--"

"Listen, Simon. Or Simonetti. Or whatever your name happens to be. I know what's going on, okay? Old Man Raguzzo--or whatever your boss calls himself--is peeved with me for all the trouble I've caused him and would love to drop me in a vat and melt me down into a sheet of plastic to cover a computer monitor. But I'm not gonna give him the pleasure. I'm just a little guy trying to make a living helping other little guys by following around petty crooks and deadbeat dads."

"You're underestimating yourself."

"Maybe. Or maybe I've got some really bright friends in high places."

Simon blinked but said nothing.

"But I've also got common sense. That's why I'm sitting here with you rather than being stuck in the ground in some fancy, overpriced pine box with a sixty-dollar garland sitting on top of it. The old man's gonna have to find smarter employees or just stop messing with people who've been around the block a couple of times. I don't intend to make his life easier by taking a stupid job in Timbuktu just because the goons he's been using aren't very bright. Get it?"

"Perfectly."

I had another slug of coffee. It was still pretty damned hot but I didn't want to finish such a terrific speech by jumping up and screaming on my way out. "Thanks for the coffee." I picked up my wraparounds and got up.

Simon also got up. "Is this how you want to end our discussion?"

"I gave you my answer. Isn't that all you wanted?"

"I would have preferred more of a discussion."

"What follows I ain't interested?"

He shook his head. "You're a very stubborn man, Mr. Deacon."

"It's the Italian in me. Or the Irish. Or the Scotch. Or German. Sometimes I get confused which part pushes around which."

I left the place. The crowds had thickened. As I headed straight for the glass doors I kept my eyes and ears alert for sudden movements and sounds.

I was about ten spaces down from the TransAm when the brunette appeared, keeping in step with my pace. She wore tight jeans, a sleeveless light-blue blouse and open-toed white pumps. "Don't start up your car."

I didn't cringe, as I should have. "I must be getting used to you."

"Did you hear what I said?"

"Were you in the restaurant?"

"Briefly. Did you hear what I said?"

A young family of four passed us. The husband carrying his toddler daughter piggyback stopped walking and stared. His wife, a skinny blond walking hand-in-hand with a boy resembling the father, also stopped.

"They let me out of the sanitarium early on good behavior," I explained to them with a pleasant wave.

"Did you hear what I just said?" my hallucination repeated.

"Yes. Where were you?"

"I was out here for a while. Then I went inside and stood right behind you until you left."

"I didn't see you."

"I didn't want you to. Did you hear what I said about your car?"

"Yes. What's up?"

"It's rigged."

"How?"

"Just take my word for it. It took them less than a minute to do it."

"Any idea who did it?"

"There were two of them. One was big, the other about your height, fortyish and skinny, with a red buzz cut. He wore thick glasses. He was the one who rigged it. The other guy stood in front of your car, reading a map."

"Clever. No one going by would ever notice."

"Why's that?"

"This is the map-reading capital of the civilized world."

She nodded. Then she was gone.

I approached the car and opened the hood. Sure enough, a wire was hooked up to the battery terminal. I unwound it, followed it beneath the body of the car, found the other end and removed it. Then I pulled it loose, wadded it up, slammed the hood shut and got in.

My pulse pounded wildly as I fired her up, but when the familiar roar of the engine pierced the silence, a wash of warm relief spilled heavily down my back.

As I pulled out of the lot, I knew one thing. Two things, actually. One: Tony Simon met with me just so their stupid goons could rig my car. And two: Old Man Raguzzo had no intention of footing the bill for my trip to Honolulu.

He sure was a cheap bastard.

Chapter 20

"A *car* bomb?"

Neil Haversack looked more perplexed than usual as he brought two coffees back to his desk. "Where the hell do those jerks think they are? Beirut?"

"Fifty cents of wire wrapped around the battery terminal, then ten feet or so running underneath, to the gas tank." I took the one he offered and blew on it. My tongue still smarted from the cup of molten lava sexy Ruthie had served me at Kenny's. I put the cup down on the edge of the desk and waited for it to cool.

"That's kind of heavy, even for Raguzzo," Neil said.

"I guess when you're old, you get so tired of irritations, you go nuclear when someone stirs the pot."

"From what we've seen and heard, the old man's mellowed over the last few years. I wouldn't think he'd want to take the heat for something like this unless he really felt threatened."

"How could a few questions about a deadbeat dad make him feel threatened?"

"Going by that car bomb, the two bozos in your apartment last night and the way you're roughed up every time you show your face, I'd say he's trying his best to let you know you're getting a little too close to his territory."

"You actually think he's taken a loser like Brandon under his wing?" The idea was inconceivable.

"Brandon might be working for him. If he is, Raguzzo won't want anyone sniffing around. You know how mob guys are."

"So he has someone rig my car?"

"Economical," Neil said.

"And cheap."

"Impossible to trace."

"Raguzzo's worth millions. He could've afforded to cough up at least a couple of grand for something like this."

Neil squinted. "You would've been more comfortable with a stick or two of C-4 hooked up to your ignition switch?"

I brought the cup to within a foot of my face. Still too hot. I put it back down and glared at it. "When you put it that way, I guess cheap was all right."

"It might not have been flashy, but it was foolproof."

"Not quite."

"Nearly impossible for anyone to spot."

"I didn't have any problem spotting it."

Neil stared at me as he drank some coffee. "That's really chafing my shorts."

"You *wanted* me to instantaneously blend in with Florida's smog problem?"

"Not what I meant."

"Go ahead and unload. You're among friends-- so to speak."

"Where was the wire?"

"I told you. It was rigged to the gas tank."

"But where *was* it?"

"Under the chassis."

"Was it pulled tight?"

"Tight?"

"As opposed to dangling loose? Hanging? Scraping the pavement?"

Neil wasn't the brightest bulb in the box but occasionally showed signs of brilliance. He'd been a cop long enough to know how to get the facts in the subtlest ways possible. He did it by asking innocent questions--just one or two, until he had the whole picture. By the time you figured out what he was doing, it was too late.

"Why's it matter?" I asked.

"Close the door."

I got up, went over and pushed it shut. Then I sat back down, picked up the steaming coffee and blew on it again. "What's on your mind?"

"I think you know."

"If I did, I wouldn't have asked."

Neil rubbed his eyes, then his brush cut. Cops didn't like it when things didn't add up. It made them nauseous and irritable. They liked things nice and simple. Complications made them worry, sit up nights and drink themselves silly. They ended up with upset stomachs and ulcers, which made them *more* nauseous and irritable.

Neil was no different.

"Deacon, something's up. You'd better let me know what it is."

182

"I wish you'd be more specific."

He leaned back. "How well do we know one another?"

"We've been friends around ten years, I guess."

"Closer to twelve."

"I wasn't counting. I was having too much fun knowing you."

He let that one go. "To put it painfully simple, look at you."

I shrugged. "I wish I could. Got a handy pocket mirror I can use?"

"You're not exactly imposing and you're not the type who can instill fear into people. Especially hoods."

"These guys are crazy. I mean certifiably psycho. You know that. I could point a twelve-gauge at most of them and they'd *still* laugh in my face."

"Point taken."

"So what is *your* point?"

"It's very simple. You're not as tough as you need to be in this business."

Now he was getting personal. "What's *that* have to do with anything?"

"You're not tough in this business, the assholes you deal with tend not to take you seriously."

"I'd rather be *deceptively* tough. Look at James Bond."

"James Bond isn't real. And even so, that's not what I mean. You're *not* deceptively tough."

"I'm tougher than I look. Take those three I handled in my office."

"It would even help the situation if you were a good shot--just in case you need to actually *use* that gun one day."

"Maybe I'll surprise you one of these days and actually hit a bull's eye."

"It would surprise me if you hit the *target*."

"That wasn't very nice. No wonder I don't remember how long we've been friends."

"Listen . . . we both know the score. You're about as non-intimidating as a private eye can be and still keep his license."

"Everyone's got shortcomings."

"Look at it from my perspective." Neil rested his elbows on the blotter. "I've got a friend who's a detective. He handles forgers, deadbeats, bail-jumpers, juvie delinks--cases that generally don't get a guy hurt or killed."

"My mother doesn't want me fighting."

"But now you're in the big leagues. The Raguzzo's, of all people. First, you get taken out at one of their tittie bars and end up in the Emergency Ward. Then three of their bone crushers pay you a visit."

"I handled that pretty well, thank you very much."

"I'm *still* trying to digest *that* one."

"Everyone's entitled to a lucky day."

"What about that cozy little party at your place last night?"

"Everyone's entitled to a lucky day."

"But when you spot a home-made bomb not even an expert from the Bomb Squad could recognize unless he was looking specifically for it, I'd call that a little *more* than a lucky day."

I shrugged. "So what's your point?" I knew what it was; I just wanted to hear him say it.

"My point is this. What the hell's *happened* to you?"

"How's that?"

"In plain English, what's happened to turn you from Joe Klutz into Sherlock Holmes in just two days?"

"Joe Klutz?"

Neil just shrugged.

"Sherlock Holmes?"

Another shrug.

I'd only had a tiny sip of coffee but felt the need to get up for a refill. It would give me time to think. I didn't know what to tell the man. I couldn't tell him a strange brunette I'd met briefly in Kelsey's men's room pops up from time to time to bail me out of some tight situations. I couldn't tell him anything else because he'd check it out. That was the most irritating thing about cops--they never believed anything you told them.

"I thought we were friends," Neil said.

"What makes you think we aren't?"

"Instead of confiding in me, you're stalling your ass off trying to think of something to tell me."

"Is it that obvious?"

"Any idiot with a working brain cell could figure it out."

I sat back down. Something came to me. It was a combination of what Phil had suggested in her office and a few things I'd been thinking about on my own. I couldn't tell Neil about the brunette or that I remembered her face but couldn't exactly place where I'd seen it. That had been bugging me more and more during the last few days, but I couldn't tell him or anyone else about it. I had to figure that out on my own.

Or ask her the next time she popped up.

But right now I had to explain all this just right, or Neil would be doubly suspicious. Cops like Neil always seemed to know when you were trying to sell them a bill of goods.

"I'm stalling because I don't know exactly how to tell you," I said.

"Tell me what?"

I put my coffee on his desk, turned around in my seat and pointed to my goose egg.

"That's where you were suckered the other night. How's it doing?"

"The swelling's down. It's just a little tender."

"Glad to hear it. Now . . . what were you about to tell me?"

I pointed to it again.

He blinked. "Are you trying to say your goose egg has something to do with all this?"

"Slightly."

"I hope you're not just stalling again."

I pointed to my head.

"*Now* what?"

"What am I pointing to now?"

He shrugged. "Your head. Or am I missing something?"

186

"No, you got it right."

"Glad to hear it. So . . . have we finished with our anatomy lesson? Or are we about to start on a nice quiet game of Charades?"

"I'm trying to tell you what happened and now you're making jokes."

"And I'm talking to the world's most serious detective, right?"

It was difficult, but I managed to keep a straight face. "For once in my life, I'm serious."

Neil threw up his arms. "Someone get Special Edition. Keep going. I'm sure Hollywood would *love* to hear this. They haven't been able to get hold of something original for years."

"This all started the night I was knocked out."

"Go on."

I took a deep breath and decided to just let him have it. "Ever since I woke up in the Emergency Room, I've been hearing voices."

He didn't laugh--as I thought he would. He leaned forward. "What . . . kind of voices?"

"They're hard to describe."

"Male or female?"

"It . . . sounds like my own voice."

"So I guess we can safely go with male?"

"You always were a good detective."

"And what does this voice tell you?"

"It tells me to watch out. It also tells me to be careful. And to check out my car before I start it up."

"Could this be your subconscious?"

"I don't know. All I know is that it's always right."

Neil sat back and scratched the back of his head. "For a while you had me worried. I thought maybe you were dealing with dangerous people for a little inside information."

"You mean an informant?"

"You did tell me you had one, didn't you?"

"I didn't know how else to explain this."

"Then you *don't* really have one."

"I don't have the money to afford one."

"True . . ."

"I'm also too chickenshit to deal with them. Some of those guys are crazy."

"I sure am relieved."

"So you don't think my hearing voices is out of the ordinary?"

"A little, maybe."

"Enough to worry about?"

"That tap on the noggin might've jarred something loose that should've been working before now. Maybe it didn't because you didn't even know it was in there."

"Does that ever happen?"

"There are all sorts of documented cases of cops--even ordinary people--taking falls or going through a serious trauma, then experiencing weird, life-enhancing episodes. Anything can happen with a head injury. Just be thankful it didn't mess up anything else."

"I'll keep you posted if I start crying when the doorbell buzzes or wet my pants if I get too close to the microwave."

"Seriously, if you have a little voice inside you that can smell trouble and helps us catch bad guys, I'd say you're a step or two ahead of the rest of us."

"So I'm off the hook, then?"

"Deacon, have you ever heard the phrase, 'get some sense pounded into you?'"

"My mother loved that. But every time Dad tried doing it to me, she got on his case."

"Well, I guess it's safe to say that it's finally caught up to you."

Chapter 21

I left the OPD building at a little past two.

As soon as I entered my Orange Avenue office, I groped for my bottle of Jack's from the bottom drawer of my desk.

I needed a good belt and a few minutes of quiet time to determine what I had to do about my present situation. I had to do all this determining right now, while the office was quiet. I couldn't handle *any* sort of serious thinking if I was interrupted in any way.

My world had gone crazy in just a couple of days. I'd been hit in the head because I went to the wrong place and roughed up because I asked questions in another wrong place.

Nothing had been right since.

I had to sit back, mellow and focus. Just forget about my hallucination and the trouble I was been having with the Raguzzo people. I needed to concentrate on what I was doing. I hadn't earned the money Sandra Brandon had given me and needed to work on the best professional way of changing that. I'd had dozens of deadbeat dad cases in the last five years and never had this much trouble with any of them. I should've already solved this one by now.

My usual jobs--delinquent fathers, missing kids--didn't pay nearly as well but didn't put you in the hospital or morgue. I'd been roughed up once or twice but had *never* found myself staring at a car bomb, or entered my apartment to find two Neanderthals right out of *Rockford Files* sprawled out on my living room sofa.

Entirely too many nasty, crazy people were making this case difficult. The more digging I did, the more nasties I found. I'd made a slew of enemies, embarrassed a crime boss, and got chummy with a dead lady.

Not bad for two days' work.

Yes, she was dead. Nothing else made sense. She popped up, told me things someone would know only if they'd actually been there, then vanished. She'd joined me at Smilin' Susie's and caused half the patrons--as well as my waitress--to stare at me as though I were crazy. She showed up in the warehouse while I was zip-tied to a chair, about to be pureed with a ball-peen hammer and caused undue stress for my torturer. She appeared in my car, my apartment, and my office.

But she couldn't be seen by anyone else.

My head injury might have opened my eyes, for all I knew. Maybe she'd been there all along. Maybe with time, I'd start seeing more dead people. Like that Bruce Willis movie about that kid who sees dead people everywhere he goes. I could hire myself out as some sort of clairvoyant and rake in the cash. If the concept wasn't so weird, I'd be more enthused.

I see Neanderthals on a daily basis.

Most important of all, I see gorgeous dead chicks.

Maybe I should have a card printed.

I was just tired.

I had a sip of Jack's, swiveled my chair around and watched the heavy Orange Avenue traffic. Sometimes watching traffic puts me into a mild state of self-hypnosis and things come to me when I don't expect them to.

But this time it didn't work. I experienced no revelation, no mind-altering experience and no subconscious explanation. Just heavy traffic and the usual activity. No dead bodies wandering around.

At least, the people I did see appeared to be alive . . .

I swiveled back around.

It only took me a second to see her standing in front of the door.

This time she wore a gold, V-necked blouse, jeans and black leather pumps. Her hair, as usual, flowed freely. In the sunlight drifting in through my office window, it appeared more chestnut than black.

She was dead, but that didn't mean she wasn't a hot number.

"Slumming again?" I quipped.

"I was just in the neighborhood, so I thought I'd stop by . . ."

I couldn't help grinning. That was one of *my* favorite lines. "Have a seat. You can sit, can't you?"

"Of course I can sit. I sat in the restaurant, didn't I?"

"Yes you did. How silly of me." I couldn't believe this conversation.

She kept her gaze on me while approaching the desk, then sat.

"It's small, but it's all mine--once the rent's paid."

She didn't respond. Sometimes my humor isn't appreciated, as it should be. Not even among dead people, apparently.

"Anything bigger or more ornate would scare away my financially-challenged clients," I explained.

Again, she said nothing.

"Drink?"

She smiled.

"Sorry. Guess I forgot."

"Forgot what? That I can't drink?"

"Short-term memory loss, apparently." I held up my glass. "Mind?"

"Not at all."

I lifted my elbow and drained what was left in the glass. Somehow, getting plastered while talking to a dead girl seemed the perfect way to while away the afternoon. I poured more Jack's into my glass. "What's your name?"

"Alicia."

I practically dropped my glass. I really didn't expect her to tell me anything. I guess this could be classified as a breakthrough.

But I forced my mind to concentrate on the conversation.

But it was difficult. In the V of her blouse, a tiny brown mole over her right breast showed on her smooth skin. Her big, beautiful almond eyes sparkled in the afternoon sunlight. I had to remind myself that, like the rest of her, the mole was an illusion. So were her sparkling almond eyes.

Hell of an illusion.

But I'd definitely seen those eyes before.

"That's it? Just Alicia? Nothing tagging along behind it?"

"Freeman."

Another ring of familiarity. "Alicia's a pretty name."

"Thank you."

"No problem. Now, Ms. Freeman--"

"Call me Mike."

"Mike?"

"My father wanted a boy."

"Where's the Alicia come from?"

"My mom's mother's name. Mike was her way of giving in to Dad."

"Why Mike?"

"The Spencer Tracy movie was one of their favorites. My dad liked golf. And Spencer Tracy."

"*Pat and Mike*?"

She nodded.

"Mike was Tracy's name, wasn't it?"

"My parents never liked Pat."

I had more Jack's and thought that over. Alicia. A beautiful name for a slender, willowy brunette with sharp features and large, haunting almond eyes.

194

Mike. A name you give your boy. Or your pet German Shepherd. Or a sports promoter played by a paunchy, middle-aged Spencer Tracy in a pleasantly funny movie made in the mid-fifties.

"All right, then . . . Mike. Call me Ralph. All my friends do. That is, if I had any."

She smiled and said nothing.

"You gonna tell me why, now?"

"Why what?"

"Why me?"

"Why you what?"

"Why all this popping up? What have I done to warrant all this attention?"

She blinked. "You don't like the attention?"

"I didn't say that."

"Then you do?"

I shrugged. "It takes some getting used to, but I'm really totally confused and a little awestruck by all this."

"Awestruck?"

"Sounds more masculine than flustered."

"It's very simple. This is all about a case you were on a few years ago."

"You'll have to be just a tad more specific."

"It was a missing person case. You were hired by a young couple to look for their ten-year-old daughter, who'd been missing for three days. She was coming home from school and someone snatched her."

"Collins." The images came back in a flurry.

The case was very unpleasant. One of my first. I'd only been a detective a few months when the call came in from Neil, who gave me a heads-up about it because he knew I needed the money.

The girl was snatched by a pervert living in a high-rise off the Trail and using a rented storage locker to abuse his victims before dumping them. I tracked him down and was chasing him on the eighth floor of the high-rise when he grabbed a woman in the hall, dragged her out to the fire escape and forced her out the window with him.

I had another slug of Jack's. "I . . . didn't solve it."

"You would have . . . if he hadn't grabbed that woman."

"Things happen. OPD nailed his ass later on, but they didn't find the little girl in time."

"And the woman he took to the fire escape--"

"She died, too." The images swept unmercifully through me.

"But at least you tried to save her."

The case still haunted me. The little girl was dead because I couldn't find her in time and the woman was dead because I wasn't able to get a good enough grip on her hand to pull her up from the balcony railing. An innocent woman who just happened to be coming out of her room at that same time.

"He got away," I said, mostly to myself.

"Yes."

"It wasn't my day."

"Wasn't mine, either." Her almond eyes, which had only been an illusion a moment ago, filled with tears that looked very real.

Then I knew. The image registered like a jolt of ice water to the face. Those eyes were the last glimpse of her I saw as she broke my grip and fell the eight stories to her death.

"You're . . . *her*?"

She nodded.

Chapter 22

After Mike left, I sat there in a daze, trying to digest, through my alcohol-induced numbness, what just happened.

Alicia Freeman. The woman I tried to save five years ago, when a pervert grabbed her and pushed her over a fire escape just before he ran down the stairs.

A woman I tried like hell to save.

A woman who fell anyway. And died.

She'd come back. I don't know how, but she had.

I remembered her face just before our grip broke. The second our eyes met just before her fall. The sheer white panic in her face. The paleness. The tear-stained cheeks. The wide-open eyes.

It was an image that would stay with me the rest of my life.

My phone rang.

Back to reality . . .

Phone. Office. A business to run.

Ralph Deacon, Private Detective. No job too big--remember?

Alicia. Her fall. That all happened before. Years ago.

This is now, remember?

I picked it up and sat there, staring at the door, half-expecting her to reappear.

"Mr. Deacon? Tony Simon."

It took me a few seconds to pull myself out of the darkness and force my head back into the late afternoon Florida sunlight. Remnants of my consciousness still clung to that balcony. I supposed they always would.

"Mr. Deacon?"

Tony Simon. Remember him? The impeccably dressed dipshit that kept you occupied while two of his cronies rigged your car to rain metal and bits of what used to be your body all over Florida Mall's enormous parking lot?

Despite the dwindling memories of Alicia, my amiable persona fluttered back in tiny waves. It might be clever to show him I was above holding a grudge. An important rule for a private eye was that it was never a good idea to let the opposition know what you were thinking or planning.

Besides, he might not have even known about the car bomb. It was unlikely, but possible. I wanted to give him the benefit of the doubt anyway. There was already too much suspicion and distrust in the world.

"I'd know your voice anywhere," I said amiably.

"You're back to your usual jovial self, obviously."

"Surviving a car-bombing agrees with me."

I heard him sigh. He said nothing.

"I'll bet things are cheerful and bubbly where you are right now. I don't hear people laughing or popping open the champagne in the background, but your office might have better acoustics than what I'm used to."

"Mr. Deacon, I hope you realize how much trouble you've caused."

"Isn't that just awful how my irritating habit of staying alive pisses off so many people?"

"That isn't what I meant."

I put him on speaker so I could pour another swallow of Jack's. I'd had quite a bit when Mike was here but wanted a little more anyway. Nearly getting blown up changes your priorities a tad. So does talking to the woman whose life you couldn't save. And especially to the man responsible for keeping you away from your car while it was being rigged.

"I understand," I said.

"Do you?" He sounded skeptical.

"Of course. I didn't let myself become part of the atmosphere and this pisses off your bosses. But I really don't care. You see, I've always been ecology minded. The constant Florida traffic has seriously messed up our clean air. I'd really feel guilty about adding to it. I'd be dead, but I'd still feel guilty. Don't ask me to explain that."

"I honestly had no idea that was going on during our chat."

"I really had to pass on letting it happen. I hope everyone understands. I've got bills to pay, cases to solve and a bevy of gorgeous women who are sitting by the phone, patiently waiting for my call. I'm also trying to save up for the down payment on that bungalow in Malibu I've been lusting over since I saw that beach movie marathon on TBS last year."

"Mr. Deacon--"

"Getting blown up just doesn't appeal to me. At least it didn't this morning. But call me tomorrow. I might have a different outlook on life."

"Listen . . . Mr. Deacon . . . may I call you Rafaello?"

God, I hated that name. The only people who wanted to call me that were Italians. No one else could even pronounce it correctly. "No, you certainly may not."

"It's your name, is it not?"

"The name is *Ralph*. At least, to my friends. If I had any."

"Ralph--"

"Mr. Deacon, to folks like you."

A sigh. "I honestly *did not know* what was going on."

He sounded sincere, but it was my duty to make him uncomfortable. If I'd already made his boss and half a dozen brainless goons uncomfortable, I shouldn't stop with Simon. When I was on a roll, I liked to see how far it could take me.

Besides, I excelled at making people uncomfortable.

I also liked it.

"It almost got me splattered all over Orange County. I might have made it to the Osceola County line if the breeze had been stronger and coming in more from the north."

"I understand if you choose not to believe me. I probably wouldn't if I were you. But as bad as that experience was, something positive has resulted because of it."

"I know. I wasn't blown up."

"Besides that, of course."

"Neither was my classic car."

"Even better than that."

"I'm listening."

"My employer is very impressed with how you handle yourself and would like to talk to you personally at your earliest convenience."

"Is this the same guy who ordered me to vaporize with that fifty-cent bomb?"

"He doesn't usually ask me to arrange such meetings. It is quite an honor."

"I guess your boss would've sprung for a much more expensive contraption if he'd known I was a crackerjack sleuth."

"Mr. Deacon, what do you say?"

"To what? My being a crackerjack sleuth?"

"A meeting with my employer."

"If he wants me dead, doing it himself would be much more honorable. Not very bright, but more honorable. At least I wouldn't talk about him like I've been doing or make jokes about those tiny-brained muscleheads who watch over his tittie bars. But I have to admit these jokes have made me popular at the local supermarket."

"I have instructions to arrange for this meeting exactly as you order it. I also have instructions to pay you for your time."

I sat back and tried to digest that last statement. Pay. That meant money. A cheap bastard like Raguzzo would only pay for such a meeting if he was really inconvenienced and angry. And if he'd already lost money.

I must have really screwed up something important . . .

"*Pay*? As in cash *money*?"

"You're to receive one thousand dollars for every fifteen minutes of your time once the meeting begins."

"You're kidding."

"Totally serious."

A thousand bucks every fifteen minutes. That was serious cash. Almost in the same league as professional boxers. Or that latest crop of Hollywood big shots.

But it sounded too good to be true.

Raguzzo obviously wanted to see me. I didn't believe the bit about that much money, but I knew better than argue with Simon about it and arouse further suspicions. If Raguzzo was determined enough to dangle such a huge carrot, I should at least act the part of the greedy private eye.

Not doing so would make him suspicious. It might even piss him off enough to cause him to make even bigger mistakes.

"That could add up to a healthy chunk--that is, *if* I choose to attend. And maybe even talk or ask questions while I'm there."

"I'm to give you twenty-four hours to make up your mind."

"And if I choose *not* to meet him?"

"The decision is yours. But if you want my opinion, I'd agree to it."

"Why? So you stay out of trouble?"

"Actually, meeting with him might keep *you* out of trouble."

"How?"

"Like I said, he's impressed with how you handle yourself. Take my word for it, he isn't easily impressed."

"So the meeting's another way to keep me out of his hair?"

"I'm not at liberty to say."

"What *are* you at liberty to say?"

"I've already said what I've been instructed to say. I'll call you twenty-four hours from now--"

"I don't need twenty-four hours. I'll talk to him. Tonight all right?"

Silence. I knew right then that I'd confused the man. I could almost see him staring at the phone and scratching his head. But being careful not to muss his hair, of course.

"Still there?"

"I . . . didn't think you'd agree this easily."

"I'm a practical man. With bills to pay."

"You're also full of surprises."

"That's one of the main reasons why my ex divorced me. But getting back to your boss. A sixty-minute meeting would make for a nice chunk of change. I can give him an hour of my time. Maybe even longer, if we both decide we're getting along and want to go the distance with a little male-bonding."

"Excellent. Want to make the arrangements now? Or sometime later?"

"Call me back in half an hour."

I hung up and had another swig of Jack's.

And thought about the next round of bullshit Raguzzo had planned for me.

Chapter 23

I spent the next half-hour watching the heaviest part of rush hour roaring past my window while trying to determine what disturbed me so much about Tony Simon's phone call.

When you're an experienced, top-notch private eye, you develop a certain feeling about everything--especially when something doesn't add up. You also develop a sense of *wrong* that flares up when something just doesn't make sense.

For one thing, I couldn't believe an important man like Raguzzo would even agree to meet me in the first place. Raguzzo dealt with corporate leaders, investors, politicians, millionaires, lawyers and other highly successful crooks. Scheduling a private meeting with a small-time detective who'd been nosing around his territory wouldn't be a key item on a big-time mob boss's list of priorities. A man like Raguzzo would more likely have one of his representatives buy me off or do me in. If that didn't work, he'd simply pay some out-of-town hitter to take me out of the picture.

Raguzzo, like most other high profilers, valued his privacy--which was the primary reason he spent most of his time at his heavily guarded mansion near Sable Point. It also explained why he rarely left his place, and when he did, traveled in armored limousines and private planes. Business associates, rivals and competitors were brought to him. He wouldn't leave the security and comfort of his multi-million-dollar kingdom to have coffee in public with someone who'd been sniffing around one of his little bars the last few days.

And even if he agreed to such a meeting, would he offer me such an outrageous sum for the inconvenience? Millionaires were crazy, arrogant and narcissistic. In most cases, they were more psychotic than the rest of the population. But they seldom tossed away money foolishly. Raguzzo was obsessively cautious and often cut corners, such as paying good money to have someone rig a fifty-cent car bomb. He wouldn't think twice about paying a couple of million for a custom Lamborghini one of his girlfriends could use to dash off to the local salon, or twenty-five grand for a limited edition Pedersoli or Berardinelli double barrel he could mount on the wall of his study . . .

But paying me a small fortune for the pleasure of my company just hours after he'd paid a hitter a small fortune to blow me up?

If he did, he was even crazier than I thought.

If this meeting actually *was* on the up and up, I had much to worry about. No matter where we decided to meet, soldiers would be standing by. There might even be a hitter or two hiding in the shadows just in case my dinner date wanted me taken out anyway. This would probably happen just before or just after the meeting. Raguzzo was always fanatically careful to be miles away during a hit. He wouldn't become reckless in his twilight years. As long as I stayed close to him, I'd be safe.

Even so, I'd have to be particularly cautious about what I said and did. I couldn't make any sudden moves. And I certainly shouldn't be surprised if someone was instructed to pat me down first. Which meant leaving my gun behind.

And when you're about to meet someone with the power to do you in with a slight nod or barely noticeable tilt of the head, you definitely want firepower as accessible as possible.

"Don't you think that's right?" I asked Mike without turning in my seat.

No reply.

I swiveled around and stared stupidly at my empty office.

I'd fully expected her to reappear and talk to me about this. She might actually be able to shed some light on it. She obviously knew a helluva lot more about what was going on than I did.

And why shouldn't she? She was dead. A spirit. She no longer had to worry about cars, buses, or trains. She could get around much easier than the rest of us. For all I knew, she might be at Raguzzo's castle right this moment, listening to what was going on.

But I couldn't rely on her for everything. What sort of private eye relies on anything but his own senses to work a case? Not exactly the sort pulling in four big ones a day and riding around in a Cadillac.

My phone buzzed exactly half an hour after my talk with Simon.

"Have you decided?" he asked.

I decided to let my powers of deduction, instinct and reasoning guide me through this one. They'd done a fairly good job so far, hadn't they? I'd come this far without anyone's help before--why should I suddenly feel the need to consult with a hallucination?

"Sure have," I told Simon.

"Well?" He sounded anxious. This situation had undoubtedly stressed him out.

"Colonial Drive seems to be a good bet for something like this."

"Why Colonial?"

I knew the area pretty well. I could easily find places to hide or disappear quickly, if I had to. I also knew which streets to avoid and which alleys led to stores and restaurants. Colonial was not an area where Raguzzo's men could move around freely. They'd have to contend with wandering tourists, hungry locals and fanatic shoppers. I couldn't think of a better place for a rendezvous with someone who might silently order one of his men to dispose of me.

"It's close and convenient," I told Simon.

"Where on Colonial?"

"There's a steak place on the north side, one block west of Maguire."

"You want to meet in the restaurant?"

"I didn't say that."

A pause. "What's on your mind, Mr. Deacon?"

"If I told you, it would ruin the surprise."

He gave a deep sigh. "I honestly hope you're not planning anything stupid."

"Me? Stupid?"

His silence was undoubtedly his sophisticated way of agreeing with me without coming down to my level.

"Bear in mind that I'm a crackerjack private eye."

"Granted."

"Also bear in mind that my being a crackerjack private eye requires me to do what I feel is necessary for my survival."

"I understand your position."

"I'll be waiting for him there."

"Inside the restaurant?"

"In the parking lot."

"I feel it only fair to warn you that he might not agree to this."

"I don't see why not."

"He doesn't make it a practice of conducting his affairs out in the open. Surely you can understand that."

"Could it be because he might feel threatened?"

"Precisely."

"Of course. What was I thinking? Someone might want to blow up his car."

Silence.

"Just tell him it's the only way I'll agree to meet him."

"If he accepts your terms, what time should we be there?"

"One hour from now."

"That doesn't give me much time."

"That's the idea, grasshopper."

"I can't say that I blame you for being so distrustful."

"Can't help it. I've seen too much corruption and dishonesty. It's tainted my soul and darkened my perception of the human condition. That car bomb hasn't exactly improved my outlook."

"I fully understand."

"By the way, if I see anyone else, the deal's off."

"My employer doesn't drive . . ."

"I don't blame him. Too many idiots, morons and lost tourists cluttering the roads."

"I'm telling you this so you won't be suspicious when you see one or two other people in the limousine."

"No problem. I'm in a generous mood."

"All right. If he agrees, he'll be there in an hour."

"I'll stick around for five minutes. I don't intend to give anyone else a second chance to rig another bomb."

Chapter 24

A shiny black limo pulled into the Colonial Drive Steakhouse precisely one hour after my talk with Tony Simon.

My Pittsburgh Pirates cap pushed down, I sat in the TransAm in the end parking space, watching for signs of possible ambush.

From my vantage point, I had a pretty good panoramic view of Colonial and the side streets on either side of the restaurant parking lot. I hadn't seen anything so far, but with mob guys you could never tell. They knew how to sneak around. They were also good at blending in. Bad guys in real life didn't look anything like movie villains. They didn't wear black and didn't favor Jack Palance, Charles Bronson or any of the latest bumper crops of anti-heroes. Nowadays they resembled Bob Newhart, Jay Leno or even the Garden Guy. I'd even seen one or two who could pass for Al Gore.

The driver opened the door, got out and pulled open the back door.

I stiffened in my seat.

The man emerging from the back of the limo was *not* Old Man Raguzzo.

Raguzzo was a short, pot-bellied man who smoked big cigars and hated wearing ties and dressing up. He was over seventy, nearly bald and could pass for the actor Robert Loggia, with the same throaty voice. That irritated me because I really liked Robert Loggia. He was great in

Scarface and the old *T.H.E. Cat* series in the sixties. I even saw him in a *Monk* episode.

This man was around fifty-five, tall and slender, with curly gray hair, sunken cheeks and sharp, foxlike features. He wore a dark two-piece suit and smoked a cigarette. The long, beaky nose told me he was probably Italian. He had the definite look of superiority about him.

I started the engine right up. I was ready to tear out of the lot and join the traffic heading west on Colonial.

The man turned sharply and waved. The driver watched me as well. Then they started moving in my direction.

Despite my growing fear, my strong impulse to slam the gas pedal to the floor, I rolled down the window. Since my strange encounters with Mike, my sixth sense had somehow intensified. I don't know if that was the result of the tap to my skull or how Mr. Personality had stuffed my brains back in. Whatever the reason, I didn't have the urge to bolt. There wasn't as much of a feeling of terror or panic as there should have been.

The two men stopped about ten feet from my window.

The gray-haired guy said, "Mister Deacon?"

"Guilty."

He shrugged. "You gonna tell me what to do next?"

"That depends."

"On what?"

"On who you are."

He chuckled softly. Then turned to his driver and barked something in Italian. The driver marched right back to the limo and got in. The gray-haired guy circled the TransAm, opened the passenger door and slid in beside me. The strong scent of his minty cologne quickly filled the cab. I left the window rolled down for fresh air. And for possible quick escape.

"Is this where we talk?" he asked.

"It's cozy and warm. My home away from home. I feel safe."

"You *should* feel safe."

The Beretta sat hidden in the console between us, but I wouldn't be able to get to it without him getting curious and asking me what I was doing.

"I agree," I said nervously.

"Just two *paisanos* talking to one another, right?"

"I don't know you well enough to call you a *paisano*--"

"Maybe after we talk . . ."

"Maybe." But something about him made me uneasy.

"I usually prefer a little *vino* and a more pleasant, relaxed atmosphere when I chat. It breaks the ice, makes everyone more comfortable. It's pleasant."

"So I take it you don't like my ride?"

He shrugged. "It's a very nice classic machine, but you wouldn't happen to have a bottle of port in here somewhere, would you?"

"I had no idea I'd need to bring anything but myself for this little picnic."

"That is most unfortunate. Since our talk might take some time--"

"I know a good place. They even have wine there, as I recall. And it isn't far."

"That pleases me." He nodded. "I'll let you do the honors."

"Could you possibly do a small favor for me first?"

"That depends what it is."

"Tell me who you are."

"My apologies. I am Salvatore Donora. My friends call me Sal."

"I knew you weren't Old Man Raguzzo."

"Yes. We look nothing alike."

"That was pretty clear, even from a distance."

"What was your first clue?"

"You're younger, taller and more distinguished-looking. You also dress better and have more hair."

"I take it you know what the old man looks like."

"Only from a distance."

"Of course. That privacy madness of his."

"He has a fear of crowds. And publicity."

"An obsession, actually."

"I can't blame him. People are assholes. When they get together, they're scary. They scare the hell out of me."

"The man has made many enemies. A crowd would be an excellent way of getting rid of him."

"I guess that's why Simon said Raguzzo wouldn't go for a meeting like this."

He seemed surprised. "Simon *told* you that?"

"He said his employer might not agree to this."

"But he didn't mention him by name."

"I just assumed he was referring to Raguzzo."

Donora chuckled. "You assume, you--"

"Make an ass of you and me. Yeah, I've heard that once or twice before."

"Let's go to your place and have our *vino*. We need to clear up a few things."

***

Novello's *Ristorante* is a quiet little place one block west of the Steakhouse, just a short jaunt from the Chinese community that had taken over that section of town during the last thirty years.

Novello's front entrance resembles an Italian sidewalk courtyard--cobblestones, umbrellas and small circular tables.

Inside the cool candlelit room, Salvatore Donora clicked his fingers just as Tony Simon had done at Kenny's earlier that day. A host, waitress and wine steward appeared at the same time--as if by magic. I made a mental note to ask him how he did that and vowed to practice it religiously until I had it down.

You never knew when a little respect might come in handy.

Especially in a restaurant, where you're used to waitresses rushing past your table to eagerly wait on the party at the next table that showed up long after you did.

But it bothered me that Donora knew his way around. It made me feel less in control of the situation. As if he'd somehow known we were coming here. I'd brought him here without any sort of warning and he acted as if he owned the place.

"You *know* this place?" I asked.

He grinned sheepishly. "I've been here once or twice before."

Right, I thought uneasily. *And Donora's driver is just a driver.*

They showed us to a corner table toward the back, where only two other tables were occupied-- one by a young family of four, the other by an elderly couple.

The family could pass as a modernized version of the Cleavers and the elderly couple a facsimile of my ex-wife's ancient grandparents, but I was still uneasy about all this and wouldn't start breathing again until I left.

That is, if I was capable of breathing again.

The wine steward appeared with the wine list but Donora barked something in rapid Italian and the steward bolted away like a gunshot.

I also needed to learn Italian. My mother tried teaching me some words a couple of times when I was a kid, but I was more interested in climbing trees and acting stupid. If my lack of the Italian language got me into trouble tonight, my tree-climbing skills might come in handy if I had to elude a few mob guys.

But I didn't remember many trees in this area . . .

"I took the liberty of ordering a vintage port," Donora said. "A nice, understated *vino* made in Lombardy in the early sixties. If that's acceptable with you."

"That's fine." I knew I should tell him I drank only Jack Daniel's but I didn't want him to think of me as some sort of cheap date. I also didn't want him to know that I had no idea what understated meant.

Donora lit a fresh cigarette. "This place reminds me of a small sidewalk café I visit almost daily in downtown Napoli. Ever been there?"

"Where? The small sidewalk café?"

"Napoli."

"Never."

"Really?"

"I never go to other countries. Too many foreigners. Florida's bad enough."

Donora swatted me on the shoulder. "You are a card, *paisano*."

"I know. A real joker." I didn't want to waste time with small talk. I came here for one reason and I didn't like it that my companion wasn't the man I'd been expecting. Or that he was obviously on his own turf.

I also noticed that he hadn't mentioned my thousand-dollar chatting fee. I wanted to mention it but thought it would be tacky. I promised myself to mention it later.

"You haven't told me why you're not Old Man Raguzzo."

"We are who we are." Donora blew a thick burst of smoke toward the beamed ceiling.

His evasiveness wasn't exactly scoring points with me. I tried a stab at subtlety. Subtlety didn't work on most people, but every once in a while you got lucky. "It's not every day I can sit at a table and listen to mindless philosophical chatter from someone I know nothing about."

"Life is full of surprises," he said with a grin.

So much for subtlety.

I wanted to slap him and see how many goons would ooze out of the stained woodwork. Then I decided to remain calm, reserved and charming. James Bond would've done the same. James Bond was my childhood idol. He was cool even when the situation didn't call for it.

"I'm trying really hard to get used to the idea that you're not Raguzzo," I said.

Donora laughed. "*Paisano*, you need to get that *sfachim* out of your mind."

I knew exactly what *sfachim* meant. My mother used it whenever I pissed her off--which was often, especially during my early teen years, when I was discovering who I was and how much I could get away with.

It wasn't exactly a pet name.

But it made me wonder just how Donora could talk about Raguzzo so candidly.

"I take it you're not the number one guy on the old man's rah-rah team," I said.

"Mr. Deacon, let me get this out in the open. I'm about to become the old man's successor."

"Really? Wow . . ." Didn't see *that* one coming . . .

"I'm here to take over his operation and I intend to do it very quickly."

"That's pretty ambitious. You have any idea how long Raguzzo's been here in Orlando?"

"Nearly twenty years. Yes. I know all about the man. He started having problems in Miami in the early eighties, right after the giant Cuban flotilla. When he realized Italians would soon be overrun, he scrambled up here like a frightened child."

"He's been doing a booming business here ever since."

"He's done very well with the drugs, the hookers and the gambling. But his day has come and he needs to step down. He's--how do you say?--much too long in the tooth."

The wine steward brought a bottle and two glasses. He poured and waited. Donora sipped and nodded his approval. The wine steward nodded in return and disappeared again. I had a sip but it was a tad sweet for my taste. I told him it was perfect. My mother would be proud. She always taught me to respect my elders.

"I take it Raguzzo doesn't know about your big plan yet."

"He soon will."

"You're not gonna start a war, are you? In Tourist Town, U.S.A.?"

"*Paisano*, I don't *need* to start a war. You've arranged it for me."

"*Moi*?" Didn't see *that* one coming, either. "And how did I do *that*? Did I pull something important without meaning to? I can't remember. Maybe this tap to the back of my head did more damage than I thought."

"Doing what you've done the last two days has severely compromised the old man's operation. Raguzzo's already talking about stepping down."

I had more wine. It was much easier to swallow than Donora's last statement.

"You look--what's the correct term?-- skeptical."

"Only because I am."

"You underestimate yourself."

"I'm trying to track down a deadbeat who's obviously forgotten or doesn't care that he has a kid to take care of. I can't help it if his buddies keep trying to protect him."

"Look at it from this perspective, *paisano*. You're responsible for several of Raguzzo's men being arrested. His business has been interrupted. He's lost money. He couldn't even find someone capable enough to do you in. And since no one ever heard of you before all this, you know how this makes him look?"

I tried a gamble. "Bad?"

"Keep going."

"*Real* bad?"

"A dickhead, actually."

"Really?"

"Worse. An *incompetent* dickhead."

I had more wine. Donora replenished my glass as soon as I put it down. It was stronger than I'd realized.

"You see, *paisano*, when you run an organization, you have to be both tough and brilliant. When you make mistakes, they'd better be little ones. You make big ones? People laugh at you. People laugh? You lose your power, your respect. Once you've lost that, you've lost everything. Then you find the nearest rock, hide and wait for the competition to take over. Then you can crawl away like a dying animal."

I had more wine. The room had grown warmer. "I never looked at it that way."

"That is because you're not a boss."

I sat back and rubbed my eyes. "I think I need to make a stop."

"I thought you were Italian."

"What's that have to do with my bladder wanting to burst wide open? Don't Italians piss like everyone else?"

"Italians know how to hold their *vino*."

"I prefer donating all my *vino* to Orlando's sewer system. I always was a huge contributor to worthy causes. You know--St. Jude, abandoned dogs, clean air, the sewer system. Besides, I'm only partly Italian. The really important part of me drinks Jack Daniel's."

I squeezed out of the booth and staggered down the hall on unsteady legs. It was dark, but I could make out the overhead lights and the square white signs beneath them that said *SENORS* and *SENORAS*.

This was ridiculous. I was a much better drinker than this. Jack's definitely contained more alcohol than port wine. I wondered if this had anything to do with all the Jack's I'd had when I was talking to the lovely dead Mike in my office.

I made a beeline for the sink, pouring cold water, cupping it in my hands and forcing it in my face. A rush of icy brilliance cascaded down my cheeks, making me shiver. "Damn," I muttered, and doused my face with another chilly deluge.

"Damn is right," a soft voice said somewhere behind me.

I spun around. Mike stood right behind me in her loose-fitting crop top, tan Capri's and red pumps. Looking as vulnerable--and as real--as ever.

"Did you spend most of your time in men's rooms when you were alive?" I asked. I couldn't help it. My curiosity was killing me.

"Actually, stuff like this is new for me."

"Not *that* new. Remember the first time we met? No candlelight, no champagne and no romantic music. Just a mix of some seriously godawful smells, scuffed linoleum, a filthy urinal and some bad guys rushing in to ruin our little party."

"I remember perfectly. What are you doing, by the way?"

"What's it look like?"

"Looks like you're getting water all over your face and shirt."

"I'm trying to sober up."

"Why are you drinking so much?"

"I've had less than half a glass, but it feels like I've sucked down a full bottle."

"You know who that man is, don't you?"

"Says his name's Salvatore Donora. We're having a nice, friendly chat out there in the dining room. He also says he's about to take over Raguzzo's organization. And all because of me."

"Salvatore Donora's dead."

"Dead?"

"For quite a while."

"You mean he's like you?"

"Not quite."

"In other words, Donora's dead, but he's out there, *alive* as well?"

"The man out there is *not* Donora."

It hit me hard.

Damn. Damn, damn, *damn* . . . "I *knew* this meeting was bogus."

"Would you like to know who that man is?"

"Do you know?"

She nodded.

"Since you're here, you might as well tell me. That is, if it's important."

"His name is Giuseppe Bacca."

"Never heard of him."

"He's Raguzzo's number one hitter. Raguzzo brings him over here from Italy whenever he wants something special done. Bacca's the best. From what I heard, he earns upwards of a hundred thousand dollars a hit."

"He's a *hit man*?"

Another nod.

"Isn't he . . . kind of *old* for that? He's got to be pushing *sixty*."

"Apparently he's really good. He's *so* good, in fact, no one has anything on him. Bacca likes using the names of his victims as aliases. It's a trademark of his."

"Why?"

"He thinks it's amusing."

"I can hardly control myself from laughing to death."

"I don't think that's how he's planning yours."

Once again I felt like an idiot. "Dammit . . . I'm being set up *again*."

"I think you need to find some way of getting out of here. Now."

I was suddenly angry--at both myself and the well-dressed jerk who'd conned me into bringing him here.

"You gonna be okay?" she asked.

"Once I can find another way out. He's been feeding me port wine. It's good stuff, but strong."

"That's probably because there's something other than grapes in it."

"Great. I'm being drugged."

"Bacca's other trademark is drugging his victims. He's got pharmaceutical skills and seems to know exactly what he's doing. He uses a light sedative that's really slow acting. Eventually you'll just fall asleep. This way, he has total control over you and can dispose of you at his leisure. He's not very nice."

I felt worse than an idiot. I felt more like a kid away from home for the first time. I'd met a hit man, driven him here and let him drug me so he can take me somewhere else, slit my throat and dump me. I couldn't believe it.

"I'm on my way out right now." I quickly wiped my face with a paper towel.

"Try the window. It'll take you out to the back. No one's out there but one of the busboys. Believe me, he won't care."

"You're sure?"

She disappeared without another word.

Chapter 25

The window above the toilet worked, thank God.

It obviously hadn't been used in a while, but after a few panic-driven heaves on my part, it opened about a foot. Using the tank for balance, I squeezed through and dropped to the ground just five feet below the window.

Novello's rear lot, maybe twenty feet wide by seventy-five long, separated itself from the strip mall directly behind it with a five-foot wooden privacy fence. Straight ahead, two dumpsters overflowing with food tainted the air. A scrub area filled the far corner.

A busboy, as Mike had said, leaned against the wooden partition, hosing down two plastic tubs. He was tall, slender and light-haired. A crumpled joint was stuck between his lips. He glanced nonchalantly in my direction when my tennies thumped the concrete.

"Hey, man," he said with a casual shrug. That aura of apathetic emptiness so common among young people nowadays showed clearly in the glossiness of his eyes.

"And a bright and enthusiastic *hey* to you as well."

Mike was right once again. He wouldn't mention my presence to anyone. He was much too busy watching the water drip down the sides of the tubs. And, of course, smoking his home-made cigarette.

"Skipping out?"

"My date's the one with the money," I said.

"Old guy? Looks rich and talks kinda funny?"

"He's Italian."

"That other country, right?"

"Yeah. That other one."

He nodded, obviously pleased with himself for his perspicacity.

"You sure know your geography."

He shrugged. "Figured he wasn't local."

"Can't fool *you*, can we?"

He pulled in more weed. He either wasn't paying attention to our conversation or just didn't care. Recalling the few times I'd smoked grass in my youth, I knew it could be either or both. Otherwise, he might have asked why I chose to leave the premises through the bathroom window rather than using the attractive--and slightly more accessible--front entrance. I considered myself lucky that I'd caught him in the middle of his joint break.

He coughed out a cloud of heavy dark smoke and sniffed wetly. "Hit?" He held it out between his thumb and index finger. "Good Colombian, man." Looked like just one or two good hits left.

I didn't want to deprive him. Life was so cruel these days--especially for those just starting out in the professional arena. "Thanks. I'm trying to quit."

"How come?"

228

"Got to watch my figure."

"*Huh*?"

"You smoke a little weed, you get the munchies. You scarf up enough shit, you blow up like a balloon. You don't have to worry about that yet. It happens when you're older."

He nodded as if he actually understood what I'd just said. Then sucked in more smoke. He quickly forgot about me and went back to applying the hose to the dirty tubs, soaking the lattice wall first before realizing his aim was off, then eventually correcting it.

I didn't think he'd even remember our brief encounter by the time he went back inside.

I trotted along the side of the building. When I reached the end, I peered around the corner.

The driver who'd followed us from the Steakhouse had parked the limo two spaces down from my TransAm. He sat behind the wheel, looking down at his lap. He was either snoozing, playing with himself or doing his nails. On the other side of my car, a Buick or Olds sat close by, two large shadows filling the front seat. They could have been two ordinary guys coming straight from work to engage in a cozy chitchat, share a joint or enjoy a line of snort, for all I knew. Or two gays having a deep discussion about their relationship before going inside for a romantic candlelight dinner.

But it didn't matter. I wasn't about to try getting closer to the TransAm.

I didn't have much time. Bacca would be getting curious about my absence and would check out the rest room himself or have one of his men do it. He'd see the half-open window, alert the men out front and the hunt would begin.

My head was still warm from whatever he'd slipped in the wine. My temples throbbed from the excitement and the stress of the evening. I had my cell with me but knew better than use it right now. I had no idea how many more of Raguzzo's men were hanging around or where they were. A long line of parked cars extended perpendicularly from Colonial, reaching halfway to the strip mall a block north. I could use them for cover as I snuck away. Then it would be safe to call for a cab.

Getting a cab in Orlando--especially at night--is not exactly the fastest or easiest method of transportation. Or the most pleasant. In most cases you're stuck with a cabby who doesn't speak English. If you can speak fluent Nepalese, Portuguese, Chinese or Spanish, you're in business. But if you're an American whose preferred language is English, getting to your destination often becomes a rare treat.

I didn't have much choice, and anyway I was tired and groggy from whatever Bacca had put in my drink.

I had to stay alert. A top-notch private eye shines with so many negative factors working against him. He forces himself to go on even when most everyone else would give up.

I took a deep breath and shook myself. Then slapped myself harshly on the right cheek. Then on the left. It stung, opened up my sinuses and made me dizzy. It also made me feel like more of an idiot than I did for letting myself be drugged. Luckily it was dark enough where I wouldn't be easily seen. Even a native Floridian might consider it odd to see someone standing outside a restaurant, slapping himself.

My course of action was clear. I had to move, and fast. I was too far away from the office and even farther away from my apartment. Even if I did make it back to my place, I had a strong hunch these people would be waiting for me.

I decided to head for the strip mall and call for a cab from there. Phil's Winter Park condo sure seemed inviting right now. Since she'd gone back to using her maiden name, I was confident these morons didn't know about her, so I wouldn't be putting her in any danger. Hopefully, she'd feel sorry for me and would let me sack out on the couch.

I also hoped she wouldn't be entertaining anyone. I hoped that for two reasons. First of all, she might not feel sorry for me if I popped up during a romantic moment. Secondly, I felt enough of an idiot already that I didn't want to barge in on my ex-wife if she wasn't alone.

Since I was so exhausted, the idea of sneaking around her building and quietly collapsing on her patio chaise lounge seemed like a terrific career move. If Phil wasn't alone, she wouldn't be

entertaining out back. Phil hated mosquitoes and
gnats.

I was too beat and disgusted to even care what
chose to feast on my blood. If there was any justice
in the world, anything that made off with my blood
deserved to be knocked out cold.

Chapter 26

"You look terrible," Phil said.

Standing in the doorway in her oversized gray sweatshirt, blue shorts and bare feet, her hair pulled back and tied with a red darning rope, she gave me that look. It's the look all women give when they want you to know something's wrong with you but don't want to tell you what it is. Their goal is to confuse a man and make him edgy. It gives them a sort of perverted high.

"Thank you," I said.

She had a puff of her cigarette and pushed the smoke out into the warm evening air. "I mean it. You look like death warmed over."

"I guess posing for GQ or *Penthouse* right now wouldn't be such a terrific idea."

"Do you feel as bad as you look?"

I held out an arm. "Help yourself."

"I'd be too afraid your condition might be contagious."

"Didn't think you'd fall for that one. Can I come in?"

"Need you ask?"

I looked past her. "You might have company . . ."

"Not anymore."

I waited patiently for more information. I hoped she'd say her company was female. Or that if he was male, he hadn't measured up to me, so she made him leave rather than humiliate him. But she could tell me about that later. I didn't want to collapse in her doorway.

I found her living room with no problem--not even in my condition. Since the front entrance opened directly into it, getting there proved a snap. Thank God I didn't even have to use my superior detective skills. But I quickly noticed the sensation of my legs threatening to give out. When I'd stumbled out of the cab I blamed my clumsiness on the darkness and the oversized curb in front of Phil's condo entrance. Now I was wondering if Bacca's knockout drops were responsible for turning me into a staggering klutz even though it had been over an hour since my last sip of his understated port wine.

I grabbed the back of the padded armchair so I wouldn't fall onto the coffee table and upset her arrangement of flowers, scented candles and expensive hardcover art books. Phil was a neat freak and hated accidents. I wondered if she still vacuumed every day to pick up those pesky cigarette ashes she constantly dropped.

"You've had a rough night, haven't you?"

"What was your first clue?"

"You're walking as though you're trying to balance yourself on a balcony ledge. And doing a sloppy job of it."

"You know I'm afraid of heights." I collapsed into the armchair and immediately sank into its soft cushions.

"Make yourself comfortable."

"Maybe I'll just sit here and relax for a little while. Take off that annoying sweatshirt and keep me company."

"What's wrong with my sweatshirt?"

"It's covering all the good parts."

"Have I ever told you how tacky you can be at times?"

"Once or twice."

"You're even worse when you're . . . when you're whatever you are right now."

"I'm tired. Really, really tired."

"Can I get you anything?"

"Such as?"

"Warm milk? A small brandy?"

"I think I've had more than enough to drink, thanks."

"Is *that* why you're here? Because you're *drunk*?"

"I'd rather be drunk than what I *really* am."

"What *are* you?"

"Do you *really* want to know?"

"I honestly don't think I can stand the suspense much longer."

"I'm messed up, exhausted, pissed and humiliated."

"You're gonna have to explain all that."

"Give me a minute. I'm about to collect my thoughts."

"Are you *sure* I can't get you anything? A drink? Another pillow? Oxygen? An ambulance?"

"Oxygen? You mean mouth-to-mouth?"

"We're divorced, Ralph. We're not supposed to be doing stuff like that anymore."

"I won't tell if you won't."

"Tell who?"

"Anyone who might actually care."

"Even if I agree, I honestly don't think you'll be able to stay awake much longer."

"Try me. I might surprise you."

"I'm still going to have to pass."

"Give me one good reason."

She shrugged. "We're divorced."

"Details . . ."

"Isn't that what divorce is supposed to be? A separation of two people who no longer want to be together, doing things like . . . like what you're talking about?"

"*You* were the one who wanted the divorce. I was pretty content with how things were."

"You didn't fight it."

"I had a damned good reason for that, too."

"I thought it was because you didn't want to make things more difficult than they already were."

"Was that my reason?"

"That's what you said at the time. Were you lying?"

"Sorry. I guess I forgot. Right now I don't think I can remember my own name."

"I think you'd better just stay there for a while."

"I didn't mean to ruin your evening. It's just that--"

236

"I know. The bad guys have done you in. Why are you here instead of in your apartment? Or the Emergency Ward?"

"I was afraid the bad guys might be waiting for me there again."

"Again?"

"They like my couch and think I'm a terrific housekeeper."

"I can see why that would attract them. Why do you look even worse than those stupid zombies from *Night of the Living Dead*?"

"They tried drugging me earlier."

She sighed. "They spiked your drink."

"Were you there?"

"I made a simple deduction."

"You always were good. Yep . . . spiked my wine."

"I didn't know you liked wine."

"I don't."

"Then why--"

"That's what I was given."

"I see."

"You know what? I *really* don't like wine now."

"I can see why."

"You really *are* good." Damn, she'd make a good private eye. If only she could get used to the hours . . .

"Isn't that what they do in those spy flicks when they want certain information? And when they get what they want, they kill you?"

237

"I think that's pretty much what they had planned for this evening's entertainment." Her voice was growing softer. It sounded almost as good as her bedroom voice, but not quite as breathy, upset or urgent. I wondered if I was smiling. I couldn't tell; my facial muscles had gone numb.

"Why were they trying to drug you?"

"They don't want me nosing around anymore."

"Can't they just ask you to stop?"

She just wasn't getting it. Sometimes Phil could be *so* naïve. "Thugs don't work that way."

"I guess I need to brush up on my knowledge of thug behavior. One of these days, after I've just polished my nails and there's nothing worth watching on television." She sat on the couch. Through my gradually closing eyelids I could tell she was worried. "A glass of warm milk might make you feel better."

"I'll be okay. I just need to lie down."

"You already are."

I thought I was sitting. "I could've sworn this was a chair."

"It is."

Using my expert sleuthing skills, I did some quick investigating and discovered that I *was* lying in a chair. I couldn't feel the floor because my legs were dangling over an arm. My head was wedged somewhere between the other arm and the cushion, but I somehow felt really comfortable. My goose egg didn't even hurt. "I hope you weren't planning something later for the evening."

"Like I said, he already left."

238

Once again I hoped she'd elaborate, but she was too busy staring at me and smoking her cigarette. We'd played games like this before. She usually won.

"Someone in my building," she said.

"Pardon?"

"You're wondering who it is. Or was."

I shrugged.

"Admit it."

"Maybe a little."

"Satisfied?" She was obviously too tired for games this evening. I hoped that didn't mean she'd just had sex. That would *really* piss me off. She mashed her cigarette in the ashtray on the small table beside the couch.

"Would I approve?"

"Probably not."

I yawned. The heavy waves of dizziness had ebbed into the same soft shade of gray that precedes sleep. "Why not?"

"Would you approve of *any*one?"

"Nope."

"See what I mean?"

"I can't help it. I have personality flaws."

"Tell me about it."

"Maybe later, when my brain doesn't keep logging off."

"Sounds good. Practical, too."

"I always was a practical guy."

"According to who?"

"You need to do stand-up comedy."

"I don't have enough spare time to sit around, thinking up good jokes."

"I can do that for you."

"I know you can."

"You'd be a hit. Jay Leno would feel threatened."

"Actually, I think I'm too deadpan to be a comic."

"Deadpan sells."

"Some people don't like it."

My eyes closed even without my help. "You just never know . . . about people . . . nowadays."

"You can say *that* again."

"You just . . . never know--"

"I didn't mean that literally."

I yawned again. The cushions were doing a number on me.

"Have I ever told you how much I hate that profession of yours?" she asked. "Sneaking around? Getting punched? Shot at? Now *drugged*? Maybe even contacting some horrible disease?"

"Once or twice . . . especially that last year . . . we were together."

"Well, I hope you realize how serious I was. And still am."

"Isn't that why . . . we split up?"

"One of the main reasons. Funny, isn't it?"

"What's funny?"

"It's also bringing us back together."

"Funny," I said. "Very, very funny . . ."

It was also funny how far away and muffled my voice sounded . . .

240

Chapter 27

The smell of sizzling bacon, toast and coffee pulled me out of my sluggish state of unconsciousness.

I sat up. A battalion of African tribal drums pounded away in my head. I gently massaged my temples and the pounding eased up. Then I lay back in the soft cushions, rubbed the sleep out of my eyes and used my sleuthing skills to determine where I was.

Someone's living room. A big, flowery, overstuffed armchair had me trapped in its soft, smothering fist. On the wall above the large European-looking couch, two framed watercolors of squiggly black lines and light-blue colors added contrast to the soft orange wall. The porcelain lamps standing boldly on the two end tables looked expensive. So did the end tables. A stack of art books, an arrangement of fresh roses and several scented candles decorated the polished mahogany coffee table filling the space between my chair and the couch.

A cloud of cigarette smoke drifting lazily by made my eyes water.

My memory cleared. I'd spent the night at Phil's.

"You okay?" whispered the soft voice inches from my ear.

Mike was standing beside the chair in her tank top and jeans.

"I think so," I whispered back. "Am I where I think I am?"

"Your ex-wife's place."

"Then I think I'm about to die."

"Why? You're doing fine."

"I won't be if you do something like you did in her office."

"I won't."

"I'm more afraid of this lady than I am of Raguzzo."

"How come?"

"She's a woman."

Mike nodded.

"Why'd you pop up? Don't tell me some of those glandular cases are on their way *here* . . ." The very thoughts of Raguzzo's men involving my ex-wife in this mess forced me alert.

"Don't worry. They don't know about her."

"You're sure?"

She nodded.

"Then why are you here?"

"I was worried. You didn't look very good last night."

"That might have had something to do with the knockout drops I had with my wine."

"Anyway, I just wanted to--"

The sound of something dropping sharply onto the stove forced my brain to concentrate on more important matters.

"Stay here. I think I'd better make an appearance." Squirming free of the red checkered blanket and tan cushions and mindful of the painful thumping in my head--as well as the dead brunette standing in my ex's living room--I shuffled through the doorway and sat down carefully on a barstool at the open counter separating the dining room from the kitchen.

Amidst clinging tendrils of cigarette smoke, Phil tended to the skillet. She wore the red bathrobe I'd given her for a birthday present several years ago. It was tied snugly around her waist. I'd selected the robe specifically because of its short length. It enabled me to enjoy an eye-opening view of her shapely calves as well as a pleasant peek at her slender thighs. Her hair was pulled back and tied. As always, she was in her bare feet. Phil never wore shoes at home unless she was entertaining.

"You're up," she said, flipping an egg.

"I never could fool you, could I?"

"You live with a private detective for fifteen years, some of it rubs off. Feeling better?"

"Than what?"

"Last night."

Mike moved over to the side, near the dining room window.

"Apparently I was able to make the long trek from the living room without incident." I tried to keep my attention on Phil and away from Mike. "I guess that's *some*thing."

"A brisk cross-country jog's your next big step, then."

"Let's see what happens once I climb down off this stool first." I rubbed my eyes and tried shaking the feeling of weakness and stiff joints. "What happened?"

"You don't remember?"

"I vaguely remember coming here. Other than that, everything's foggy."

"You were dopey and hobbled around like an old man with two recent hip replacements."

"Not my usual peacock-confident strut?"

"Hardly."

"I didn't try anything, did I?"

"Such as?"

"You know. Touching? Grabbing? Maybe a wet kiss? That sort of thing?"

"You hinted at a little innocent foreplay. But like I said, you were much too busy trying to keep from falling flat on your ass."

"That's never stopped me before."

"You weren't functioning--which would've made for some hilarious bedroom entertainment. I don't know if I could've kept from laughing."

"That never stopped *you* before."

"Luckily you nodded off quickly."

Mike had left the window and was checking out the knickknacks on the shelves of the corner hutch. I wished she'd just vanish and pop up later, when no one else was around and I wasn't so nervous about what she might do.

"What do you keep looking at?" Phil asked.

My butt cheek nearly slipped off the stool. "Your tasteful décor and color sense. What did I say?"

"Pardon?"

244

"Last night."

"Before or after you nodded off?"

"Before. I don't care what I say in my sleep."

"You told me you'd been drugged."

"I *told* you that?"

"The fact that you zoned out as soon as you lay down told me *some*thing was up."

"Like I said, you'd make a good detective."

"Maybe in another life."

"I hope I wasn't much of a bother."

She slid the eggs onto a plate and brought them over with a larger plate covered with bacon strips and wedges of whole wheat toast. "I had a horrible time finding a blanket to cover you with before I went to bed. It must have taken me nearly two minutes. I'll never get them back, will I?"

"I'll make it up to you some day."

"Just so long as it doesn't include my remarrying you."

"Conditions, conditions."

Mike sat on the stool on my right. She grinned impishly but didn't say anything. Phil squashed her cigarette in the glass ashtray on the counter and sat down on my left.

I wondered if either of them had heard my sphincter pucker.

"A girl's got to have *some* boundaries," Phil said.

It took me a moment to remember what we were talking about. The familiar vanilla scent of Phil's hair, usually an instant elixir, couldn't pull my attention away from the dead woman sitting on my right.

"You heard me, didn't you?" Phil was giving me one of her quiet, probing looks.

"Sure I did."

"What did I just say?"

"Something about boundaries."

"Otherwise, a girl doesn't realize what she should or should not do."

"That's why we split up, isn't it? So you could spread your wings."

"I was spreading them with you, but only part-time."

"Your wings?"

"You can be *so* crude . . ."

I munched on a bacon strip. I kept glancing at Mike. She just sat there, watching us. I figured she wouldn't do anything to give herself away, but it was impossible to ignore her completely. Those almond eyes pulled me in like a heavy-duty magnet.

"I guess I didn't know you as well as I should have," Phil said.

"You knew me as well as anyone."

"Sort of."

"*Sort* of?"

"Living with a man and never knowing where he is or if he is going to come home alive is not the sort of relationship the average girl wants."

"I didn't realize you were the average girl."

"I was speaking metaphorically."

"Speak plain. I'm a simple country boy."

"Simple?"

I shrugged. "I can be metaphorical, too."

"I wanted a simple man with simple tastes doing a simple job that brought him home every night. Having a weekend together once or twice a year would've been nice, too."

"Doctors aren't home all the time."

"Doctors don't get drugged. Or shot at. Or beaten up."

"They get paid more, too."

She blinked. "Are you *trying* to make yourself look worse? You don't need the help."

"Occasionally you try and save someone's life," Mike whispered.

I dropped my fork. It smashed into one of my egg yolks, nearly splashing me.

"You okay?" Phil asked.

"I think so." I shot a quick glare at Mike while picking up my fork.

"Anyway, that's all in the past, so why are we even going there?"

"For old time's sake?"

"Hardly."

"So here we are, together again, enjoying breakfast and talking over the good times."

"Only because you were nearly killed and came here rather than go back to your own place and let those animals finish the job."

I ate more bacon. "I'd much rather be with you than those animals *any* day of the week."

"Then why did you spend so much more time with them than with me?"

247

"It's my job. Otherwise, I'd be with you every single moment."

"*Such* a charmer."

"I'm partly Italian. Charm comes easy."

"So when do you plan to use some of it?"

"Ouch. Once again, your feminine wit is scathing."

"I thought you admired my wit."

"It's your legs I *really* admire."

"And here I was thinking you loved me for my mind."

"I don't mind your mind. But what sort of guy worth his salt is going to admit that he's with a gorgeous woman because of her *mind*?"

"A guy with taste and intelligence?"

"I think taste and intelligence are highly overrated."

Mike laughed.

I shot her another glare and she covered her mouth and turned away.

"It shows," Phil said.

"Another ouch. And what was it about me that attracted you?"

Her sudden glare said the cute part of the conversation had just expired. "I nearly had to have therapy, Ralph."

"Nearly having therapy attracted you to me?"

"I'm serious." Her eyes turned glacial.

"Was it that bad?"

"It was either therapy or become an alcoholic."

"What's wrong with being an alcoholic? We would've been a matched set."

"Your lifestyle was killing me. I couldn't stand being home alone, waiting for the damned phone to ring. And every time it rang, my heart leaped into my throat."

"You should've gotten that West Highland terrier you always wanted. Then you would've had company."

"Then there would've been *two* of us waiting for that damned phone to ring."

"I was always careful."

"How can you be careful when you're always looking for someone who is probably a murderer, has dozens of dangerous people working for him and stands to lose everything when you find him?"

"That raises a valid point."

"Which is?"

"I wish I could think of it right now."

She picked up a piece of toast. "Those talks we had that last year?"

"Which ones? We had quite a few, as I recall."

"The ones where I discussed leaving if you didn't find another profession."

"Ah. *Those* talks."

"You apparently didn't take them seriously."

"I did at the time."

"And the other times?"

"I was hoping you were too much in love with me to leave me."

"Who drugged you, by the way?"

"An Italian gentleman."

"An Italian *gentleman*?"

249

"He dresses well, knows the best wines, speaks fluent Italian--"

"And *drugs* people?"

"He's paid to do stuff like that."

"He *drugs* people for a *living*? I've never heard of such a thing."

I didn't reply. I had a bad feeling about where this was going.

"Ralph?"

I tried busying myself with another strip of bacon. Mike was watching me, too. I felt vulnerable and ready to be skewered. For a moment I wished I could vanish like Mike.

"Why does he drug people?"

"Like I told you. He's *paid* to--"

"Why is he *paid* to drug people?"

"He's . . . a hit man."

She put down her toast. I knew I was a dead man. "You were with a *hit man*?"

"My work often requires me to come into contact with all sorts of people in *all* walks of life."

"What were you doing with *him*?"

"Having a nice, pleasant conversation."

"You can't have a nice, pleasant conversation with a *hit man*."

"Why not? They're people, too."

"Ralph Deacon, you're an idiot."

"Now you sound like one of my high school teachers. And a couple of my aunts."

She got up and stomped back into the kitchen. I could tell she was upset. Phil was usually light on her feet, except when she put on those spikes that

250

made her calves look so sensational. But right now her bare feet slapped the tile floor like a series of open fists. She poured two cups of coffee, brought them over and slid one toward me. Then she put hers down and plopped back down on her stool. "An idiot," she repeated, and took her wrath out on the poor egg yolk lying helplessly in her plate.

"Care to be more specific?"

"Don't be cute, Ralph. You came here last night because someone drugged you. Now I find out the man responsible actually *murders* people for a living. How much more specific can I be?"

"I don't see why you're so upset. I managed to give him the slip."

"What's to prevent him from following you here and killing both of us?"

"He didn't follow me."

"How do you know?"

"I'm a professional."

"But how do you *know*?"

"He didn't," Mike said.

"I know," I told her.

"What?" Phil asked.

"I said, I know. I gave him the slip."

She sighed. "How do you *know*?"

"Why do you keep asking me that?"

"Because you keep not answering me."

"I was careful."

"That *doesn't* make me feel better."

"Hit men don't work like that. He's after *me*, not you. There isn't a contract on you."

"What if he thinks I'm in his way?"

251

"Why should he think that?"

"Look at those drug people. One of them gets on a plane and his rival will blow up the plane just to make sure the first guy is dead. The *entire plane*, Ralph. Not just the seat with the victim in it."

"How can anyone blow up just one seat?"

"*Ralph* . . ."

"This is different."

"How?"

"Like I said, he didn't follow me."

"These people who are after you. Who are they?"

Now I knew our pleasant breakfast had end abruptly. "The Raguzzo's," I said after some hesitation.

Her eyes grew. "My *God*. You don't mean . . . you can't *possibly* . . ." She pushed aside her plate, put her fists in her lap and closed her eyes. She usually did that when she was ready to explode. She was probably counting to ten.

After about five seconds, she sighed deeply and opened her eyes. "In other words, you're dealing with a crime organization with political ties."

"They've got one or two."

"Which include the police."

"I'm not so sure they have as much control over the cops as they did years ago."

"But they might."

"There are dishonest people everywhere. Even among cops."

"So . . . maybe they might know someone in the DMV?"

252

I knew what she was getting at. "Possibly."

"And you don't think they can find you?"

Phil wasn't stupid, but I had to find some way to calm her down. Or at least keep her from strangling me. "They have their own code of ethics."

"Are these the same people portrayed in movies who attend church while their men are running around the city, butchering people? And dumping their bodies in the canal? And sticking horse heads in people's beds while they're sleeping? You *can't* be serious."

"Those are just movies. Everyone knows--"

"They can't *possibly* do anything violent or vicious in real life, can they?"

"Movies and the media hype everyone up. They exaggerate things."

She picked up her coffee cup. "Ralph, *please* finish your breakfast and leave."

"I think she's being melodramatic," Mike said.

"I think so, too," I whispered.

"*What*?" Phil asked.

"I think you're being a little . . . melodramatic."

"Please go now."

"That sounds so . . . final."

"So does having a hit man after you. And maybe me."

"Like I said, you're fine. You're using your maiden name again--"

"And none of them will think of looking up courthouse records? Remember what a marriage certificate looks like? In case you've forgotten, it's

253

got *two* names on it. Yours *and* mine. My *maiden* name, to be precise."

"I honestly don't think they'll go *that* far . . ."

She slid off the stool. I could tell she wanted to either get mad again or cry but couldn't decide which. "After you leave, I want you to do me a large favor."

"Sure. Just name it."

"I don't want to know if something terrible happens."

"Something . . . *terrible*?"

"Death. Murder. Dismemberment. Something along those lines."

"You mean to *me*?"

"Who else, Ralph? *I'm* not the one playing cops and robbers with psychos."

"Yep," Mike said, nodding. "Melodramatic."

I shot her another glare.

"I don't want to know if they find your body floating in Lake Eola," Phil said. "Or Lake Conway. Or any of the other dozens of lakes in Orange County."

"Phil, I really think you're taking this--"

"Write something down, have it notarized, make copies and put them somewhere in your apartment and in your office. And *please* make sure my name is *not* mentioned *anywhere* on them, OK? I don't want to be named your next of kin and I *surely* don't want you to leave me anything. Have I made myself clear?"

"Are you really sure about this?"

"Positive."

"Don't want to think it over for a--"

"I've got to get ready for work. You can find your way out, can't you?"

"If I have to."

Phil moved closer but instead of kissing me, she whispered, "You have to." Then turned to walk away.

"She's not very nice," Mike whispered behind me.

"You just don't know her like I do," I whispered back.

"What did you just say?" Phil spun back around.

"I just mumbled something about you not really wanting me to."

She smiled humorlessly. "I really want you to. Really and truly."

"Can't I stay a *little* longer?"

"What would it accomplish?"

"I'd like to see what outfit you plan to wear. Remember how you used to model for me before you--"

"Ralph, finish your breakfast and *leave*." Then she disappeared around the corner.

"See?" Mike said. "Not very nice *at all*."

Chapter 28

The Indian cab driver dropped me off in the parking lot of Novello's just before ten.

He muttered something in choppy Nepalese, grinned when I handed him a twenty, then sped off while I was waiting for my change.

Cabbies have ripped me off before. The ones sounding like they've only been in this country a few minutes learn pretty fast what it means to be a true capitalist.

I just shrugged and focused on what I had to do.

Like getting in my car and driving off without getting blown up.

First of all, I scanned the parking lot. My TransAm was the only vehicle parked in front of the place. It appeared to be unmolested. Novello's opened its doors at two o'clock. Its employees wouldn't be showing up for hours.

I checked for wires or other visible signs of disturbance before getting closer. That done, I opened the hood. I was no mechanic but knew what explosive devices looked like. Since I was parked so close to Colonial, whoever did any rigging would have to do it quickly and inconspicuously, should any cops get suspicious and come over to investigate.

No funny wires or boxes attached anywhere. No sticks of dynamite or blocks of C-4 taped to the chassis.

I carefully unlocked the door, opened it, studied the ignition and checked underneath, making sure the pedals were undisturbed and free of wires and other foreign objects. Then I twisted around to have a peek beneath the seats. Aside from my tire jack, some discarded change, a small socket set Phil bought me that I never used and half a dozen healthy dust bunnies, everything seemed all right.

I gently eased open the console. My Beretta lay in the same position. I depressed the clip, examined each bullet, and held the barrel up to the light. No obstruction. I snapped the clip back inside, pumped one into the chamber and slipped the gun into my trouser pocket. Satisfied the car wasn't touched, I fired her up and gritted my teeth. I don't know why you grit your teeth when you expect something to blow up, but it felt right, so I did it.

The powerful engine roared to life.

I was still alive. But still sweating and still suspicious. I just couldn't see Bacca having his men hunt for me without doing something evil to my car. I figured he'd be pissed for letting me slip away and would take it out on my car. I also figured Raguzzo would be pissed at Bacca for letting me slip away and would have Bacca capped for screwing up, or whatever is done to hitters when they fail to finish a job. Bacca might rig my car to get me some other way. He'd tell Raguzzo what he'd done and would remain Raguzzo's favorite hitter.

Or maybe Bacca didn't rig cars. As Mike told me, Bacca was a pharmaceutical sort of guy. Maybe he didn't work with explosives. It might wrinkle his suit.

I guess I needed to learn more about hitters. After all, I was in the profession--why not research something that just might make me a little more aware of what was going on?

I put it in gear and pulled out onto Colonial.

Not much traffic, but I carefully evaluated each passing vehicle. Most of the windows I saw were tinted. I just had to take a chance no one in my immediate area posed any sort of threat.

I crept up to the red light.

A shiny black van pulled up beside me. A middle-aged woman sat behind the wheel, inspecting her hair in her mirror. A dark-haired guy in the maroon Mustang behind me chatted with his passenger, a skinny blonde in a black tank top fluffing her hair.

The light changed.

I resumed breathing only after I proceeded on green and was reasonably confident I might not yet become a vaporized splash blending into the stratosphere.

But I couldn't stop wondering they hadn't tried getting me while I was standing outside my car.

***

My apartment complex gave no indication of disturbance.

No unfamiliar vehicles filled the spaces across the walk. The usual oldsters in white shorts and straw hats gripped their canes taking their morning stroll. No shadows lurked behind the palm trees or among the palmettos.

I cautiously approached my front door and once again prepared myself. The mat lay where it was supposed to be. The front door was locked.

But I still wasn't taking any chances.

I pressed my ear against the door and listened for a full minute.

Silence.

I pulled the Beretta out of my pocket, eased open the door and slipped inside.

The apartment was empty.

I headed straight for the bourbon bottle. Poured half a glass, took the glass and the bottle to the armchair, and collapsed in it.

I had a sip and thought about calling Sandra Brandon. She deserved to know I was making no progress whatsoever in the case. I wasn't exactly in the mood to tell her that, but it was part of the job. I figured my charm and pleasant manner might soften the blow.

It pays to be optimistic--especially in this business.

My cell buzzed.

"Rafaello Deacon?" the soft, raspy, Robert Loggia-sounding voice said.

"I go by Ralph, but you got the Deacon right."

"You ashamed of Rafaello?"

"I was in fifth grade before I could even spell it. Who *is* this? And why should *you* care which name I go by?"

A pause. "Testy, ain't we?"

"I can be . . . when the situation calls for it. Who *is* this?"

"I'm the gentleman you've been pissing off the last few days."

"I piss off lots of gentlemen. Ladies, too. Especially ladies. Pissing off gentlemen takes some thought and planning. Pissing off ladies--well, for me, it's a natural talent. I'm really good at it. Keeps the blood flowing. It's fun, too."

"You're quite the smartass, ain't you?"

"That's natural, too. Let's get back to who you are. You say I've been pissing you off. Please be more specific."

"This line clean? I got it scrambled on this end, but you never know."

"You're safe. I can't afford the technology the cops use."

"This is Papa Joe."

Raguzzo referred to himself as Papa Joe to his friends, family and business associates. He never used his last name.

"Papa *Joe*?"

"I know you heard of me. What's the problem?"

"The *pizza* guy?"

"That's Papa *John*. Idiot.*"

"You're obviously not that demented South American dictator. He's dead, isn't he? He's got a slew of kids, but--"

"Papa *Doc*, you *sfachim*."

"Ah . . . I'm back home again."

260

"Say what?"

"My mother used to call me that when I screwed up."

"Your momma, she sounds like one bright lady. She still around?"

"Not really."

"Sorry . . ."

"She has a place in Lauderdale."

I could hear him sigh. "How 'bout your old man?"

"Why? You interested in my mother?"

"Have some respect. I'm curious."

"He died about twelve years ago."

He was silent a moment. "Your momma. Someone looking after her?"

"She lives next door to her brother, his family and their nephew."

"You see her much?"

"Once in a while."

"You need to see her. She ain't getting any younger, you know."

"She'd love to hear that."

"Just facts, *paisano*. When they're gone, they're gone."

"Really?"

"Can the smartass."

"I wish I could. It's a big part of my persona."

"And a big part of my headache."

"I aim to please."

"Your momma. She needs to know how much shit her son's been causing."

"I was always her problem child."

"You been fucking up, Rafaello."

"Ralph. Like I said, please be more specific. I've got a bad memory."

"Nothing's wrong with your memory. Something tells me you're much brighter than you let on."

"I have my moments."

"Listen here . . . we got to get some things straightened out, you and me."

"Specifically?"

"You want it spelled out?"

"Please."

The old man sighed. "You *better* not be taping this . . ."

"Hey, I'm a poor, harmless dick."

"Funny. A regular clown. Pagliacci in the flesh. It's like this . . . I got businesses to run and you're fucking them up."

"It's nothing personal."

"That don't matter. I can't run my businesses with some *stronzone* slapping me in the face with his balls every time I turn around."

"Ouch. That sounds *painful*."

"It could be . . ."

"Any ideas? Every time I try doing my job, I get hit over the head or zip-tied to a chair."

"I'm running out of options, *paisano*. I do something, you get in the way. I do something else, you get in the way."

"You're forgetting one tiny detail."

"What's that?"

262

"I get in the way, you send someone to talk to me, and while we're talking, you pay someone to rig my car."

He sighed. "I was upset. I'm an old man. Life's too short. You're old and rich, you don't need fuckups. You pay somebody to make things right."

"What's wrong with saying, Oops, let's do this some other way?"

"I never said *upps* in my life."

"I believe you."

"You better."

"You didn't even pronounce it right."

"You *sure* this line ain't bugged?"

"Last I checked, it wasn't. It *should* be, but--"

"Why should it be?"

"I'm kind of pissed at you, too."

"Why you pissed at *me*? I ain't the one causing all this shit."

"I'm remembering that cozy little dinner your hitter and I had last night."

"How the hell did you know *that*?"

"Know what?"

"Who he is."

"I've got friends."

Silence.

"You stay upset, don't you?"

"Howzat?"

"Upset. You. First Simon, then your hitter."

"I like things taken care of. Neat. Clean. My business loses money with fuckups. Want to know how you can make me feel better?"

"By dying?"

"Besides that."

"Moving away?"

"That'd be nice, too."

"I like it here."

"Where? Orlando? Or living?"

"Both, actually. I'm not wild about tourists, but what the hey, I can get used to anything."

"Meet with me. We'll talk."

"*Meet* with you?"

"What I said."

"Not Tony Simon?"

"Fuck Simon."

"No, thanks. He's good-looking and neat and probably really knows how to treat his dates, but definitely not my type."

"You know what I mean, smartass."

"Not that Bacca guy?"

Another pause, this one longer. "How the *hell* do you know his name?"

"I know more than you think."

"You got friends I don't know about?"

"Sure do. So tell me about Bacca."

"What about him?"

"Will he be there?"

"He's back in Palermo, doing some business for me there."

"Good. He makes lousy drinks."

"Don't worry about him no more."

"What about the Brandon guy?"

"Who?"

264

"The man I've been looking for. He's the reason I've become a problem for you."

"Fuck him. Listen, you want to talk? We'll talk. You and me. No distractions."

"How can I be sure we'll be by ourselves?"

"You have my word. Know what that means?"

"Does it mean I'm not going to die?"

"We're all gonna die, *paisano*."

"I'm talking about years before my time. Like maybe today or tomorrow."

"You're safe while you're talking to me. You wanna meet or what?"

"Where?"

"My place."

"Which one? You have two or three."

"Eight. Eight in Orlando, that is. In Miami, I got three. In Tampa, I got--"

"You want to meet in Orlando? Or should we spend the rest of the day talking about how many places you own?"

"Dante's."

"That elegant restaurant in Winter Park no one can afford?"

"That's the one. And the prices ain't *that* high."

"Maybe not to *you* . . ."

"Been there lately?"

"I can't afford it. I'm just a poor, harmless dick."

"Crap. Meet me there tonight."

"Will I be able to get in?"

"Why wouldn't you?"

265

"The prices--"

"Fuck the prices. Everything's on me."

"As long as I don't order anything?"

"Stop being a wiseass. You wanna talk or what?"

"What time?"

"Six."

"I'll be there."

"Good. We'll talk. It'll be nice. No worries, right?"

"You make better drinks than Bacca?"

"You pick what you drink."

"Sounds good."

"I told you it'd be nice . . ."

"I'll be on my guard."

"Hey, I give you my word. *Capisc*?"

"Sure. But I'll still be on my guard."

"You don't trust me?"

"With the lives of all ten of my unborn children. But I'll still be on my guard."

Chapter 29

Dante's *Ristorante*, a big white villa topped off with an ornate red Spanish tile roof, dominated the block.

Its stucco walls, pillars and terraces belonged in Miami Beach rather than Winter Park's elite Park Avenue district.

Ceramic tile covered the floors in the dark, cool room. Wine bottles wrapped in wicker baskets hung from the stained wooden beams. Candles flickered in the center of each small round table. A p.a. system whispered soft Italian love ballads.

I went inside at around six-fifteen. I was late because I'd circled the block three times to make sure I didn't see any steroid freaks or mean-looking guys in suits wandering around. I didn't see any, but that didn't make me feel any better; it just made me wonder where they were hiding.

I also had a problem finding a parking space. The closest one was more than a block away from the restaurant--something else that didn't make me feel any better.

In the lobby, a tall, slender host around twenty-five smiled at me between two attractive, dark-haired women dressed in lacy black and white waitress uniforms that showed off their ample bosoms and fleshy thighs.

No sign of Mike.

Papa Joe, looking much older than his seventy years, sat in a corner booth. His tanned bald pate reflected the orange pinpoints of the flickering candles in front of him. He wore a tan dress shirt and black dress slacks. He never wore ties. This occasion proved no exception. He kept his shirts open at the collar and rolled up at the sleeves, giving the impression he was a working stiff who loved physical labor.

The large onyx ring nearly obscured the pinky of his left hand. A gold wedding band encompassed the appropriate finger. Like most Italians, he was big on family. He'd been married to the same woman for nearly fifty years and had six kids, most of them daughters--a fact that any self-respecting Don keeps as quiet as possible.

He wore no other jewelry. He checked his Rolex when I came in, frowned and had a swig of red wine.

The stupid-looking, broad-shouldered guy standing beside him probably served as one of his lieutenants. He watched me as a guard dog eyes the enemy getting too close to its master. I expected him to reach into his jacket or rush right over and pat me down. He remained at his post, awaiting his next command, which turned out to be very subtle. Papa Joe reached up as if brushing a fly off his cheek. The goon behind him disappeared silently.

"Deacon?" Papa Joe frowned again, tilted his head and lowered his eyes to my jacket. I suspected he was looking for signs of a gun.

"Guilty."

"You carrying?"

"I always do. Lots of psychos out there. Some even try rigging your car when you're inside, drinking lousy coffee."

"You ain't gonna use it on me, are you?" He looked worried.

"I have it for protection. I didn't get to be a detective by shooting people I don't like."

"You don't even know me."

"Maybe not, but I'm not too wild about the people who work for you."

"I'll talk to them, tell them to lay off."

"I'm still going to check my car when I leave."

He blinked. "I gave you my word."

"You said I'll be okay while I'm with you."

"I meant it, too."

"I believe you."

"Then what's the problem?"

"You said nothing about what might happen when I'm walking back to my car."

"Me, my place, my property--all the same."

He sounded sincere, but I just couldn't take the word of someone who made his millions moving cocaine, employing hookers and keeping his enemies in check by planting them in the foundation of his buildings. "My ex-wife knows I'm here."

Papa Joe's thick black brows bumped together. "You still talk to your ex-wife?"

"We're still friends."

Papa Joe shook his head. "Don't understand how you can break up with a woman you've been screwing every day and stay friends."

"It happens. But it wasn't every day."

"No?"

"Too bad. Maybe we'd still be married."

"Why wasn't it?"

"That's kind of personal."

"So why you telling me this?"

"You brought it up."

"You brought up the ex-wife part."

"She wants me to call her later tonight. She can't find an old piece of jewelry and wants me to check to see if I have it when I get home. She doesn't get the call, she's going to worry. Might even call someone to look for me."

That was a lie, but he didn't have to know that. I just thought I'd warn him in case he planned something unpleasant after our chat. He wouldn't pull something in his own place, but you just never knew about people nowadays. Raguzzo didn't get where he was by being overly generous to people causing him grief.

"Sit." He patted the cushion beside him.

I sat about three feet away from him, near the far edge. I hoped Mike wouldn't pop up. If she did, she'd have to sit between us. That would really freak me out.

I sincerely hoped she wouldn't show. That would mean Raguzzo was planning something later.

"I don't bite," the old man said.

"I'm claustrophobic."

"You no like sitting too close to another guy, right?"

"Now you got it."

270

You never knew when some gorgeous babe would want to size you up when you weren't looking.

He nodded. "Have some *vino*." He poured some from the bottle into a second glass.

I stared at it.

"You no like *vino*?"

"I no like getting drugged."

"It ain't drugged."

"How do I know?"

"I'm drinking from the same bottle."

"How do I know?"

"Want me to have a sip? Show you it's okay?"

"Be my guest."

He picked up my glass and drank. Then put it back.

I still didn't drink.

"Now what?"

"I don't like drinking from the same glass as a stranger."

Sighing tiredly, Papa Joe clicked his fingers. The wine steward instantly appeared. "Fresh glasses."

I really needed to learn how to do that.

The steward disappeared and reappeared within ten seconds. Amazing. I wondered if he could appear in two different places at the same time.

The steward poured two drinks and carefully put my glass in front of me.

I picked it up. By the time I had a sip, the steward had disappeared again.

"All right now?" Papa Joe slid closer. His arm rested on the back of the seat. He looked like he wanted to tell me a story.

"Fine." I put down the glass. The port was good and strong. If it was drugged, these guys knew their work. I'd been watching them both closely and didn't catch any sort of sleight-of-hand. But that didn't tell me anything because I hadn't seen Bacca do anything funny either.

"What's it gonna take?" Papa Joe asked.

"What's what gonna take?"

"What's it gonna take to get you to leave me and my businesses alone?"

"Not much. Just a little hush money, a winter resort in the Keys and maybe a lube job for my TransAm."

"I'm serious, Rafaello."

"Ralph. Listen, Mr. Raguzzo--"

"Call me Papa Joe."

"I'd feel funny doing that."

"Why?"

"I don't know. I'd just feel funny."

"Talk to me."

"Listen . . . Mr.--Papa Joe . . . it's like this. I never wanted to interfere with your organization."

"Go on."

"Look at me. I'm small potatoes. Bullies loved me in school. I only go to the shooting range late at night, when no one else is there. I don't like people laughing at me when I shoot out the lights."

"Cut to the chase." He drank more wine.

"I'm a klutz. An incompetent. I admit it. I go after small-time crooks because I'm too chickenshit--"

"Bullshit."

"No, chickenshit."

"No. *Bull*shit."

"Excuse me?"

"Listen, Rafaello--"

"Ralph."

He moved closer. "You gonna tell me you're a klutz when you been doing the things you been doing?"

"Like what?"

He lowered his voice. "You go into my place and ask questions."

"I was trying to find out about Brandon."

"Fuck Brandon. Why keep bringing him up?"

"It's my job to find him. But every time I ask about him, someone hits me over the head and tries doing nasty things to my body."

"Like what?"

"Like zip-tying me to a chair and playing games with me."

"Games?"

"With hammers and machetes and jumper cables."

Papa Joe shrugged. "I know nothing about shit like that."

"It happened in your place."

"Which one?"

"Vesper's."

He squinted, staring at me. I could tell he was confused. Maybe he didn't know about the zip-tie incident. Maybe he didn't even know I was there. He was a busy man. He couldn't possibly know everything his employees did. But he was still accountable for everything that went on in his places.

"What were you doing *there*?" he finally asked.

"Asking about Brandon."

"Brandon, Brandon." He tossed it aside. "Punks like him? A dime a dozen."

"I have no doubt. But when I ask about him, your employees tend to get nasty and bummed-out and upset."

"Like I said, I know nothing about shit like that. I own places. I need people to run them. I've got lots of employees, lots of associates. You go to one of my places, you deal with my guys. You piss off one of them, he reacts. He might not react the way he *should*, but if he's working at one of my places, he's probably young. Full of himself. A hot-head."

He had more wine. "But what you were saying before. Your being a klutz. You ain't no klutz. I *know* you ain't. I use good boys. There ain't no way they're gonna let themselves get their asses hauled in when they're shadowing a klutz."

"What are you trying to say?"

He lowered his voice again. "You're good, Rafaello--"

"Ralph."

"I could use a good man in my organization."

"Yeah, since the men you already have can't even follow a klutz without getting arrested."

He sighed. "One, you ain't no klutz. Two, you work for me, we both win. I get you outa my hair, you get yourself a good job. I pay well. Just ask around."

"Who should I ask?"

"Anyone who works for me."

"And they're supposed to say what? That you pay well?"

"They will. 'Cause I do."

"And if they say no?"

"They won't."

"Because they'll end up dead?"

"I pay top wages. That's why they stick around. One big happy family. You come work for me. You'll see what I mean."

"Doing what?"

He shrugged. "Whatever you want. You wanna keep doing what you do? People owe me money and skip town all the time. Go find them and bring them in. I'll match what you're being paid right now, only you'll be paid even when you're *not* looking for anybody. You're on straight salary, you get paid every Friday. You wanna run one of my places? That's fine, too. I got eight clubs around here. I also got a couple in Tampa and a few in Miami. I'll send you wherever you wanna go."

"In a pine box?"

"You're a good kid, Rafaello--"

"Ralph."

"I like good kids. I like kids that respect their mommas. Be a shame to stick you in a pine box. I respect quality. I reward quality. No reason I should have someone take you out--not when we can work together. *Capisc?*"

"What if I say no?"

"To what?"

"Working for you."

"You no wanna work for me?"

"I don't think so."

"Why the hell not?"

No need to get him worked up again--especially since we were having such a nice friendly chat and he kept hinting that he didn't want me killed. I didn't want him to change his mind. I still had to leave this place, find my car and drive the twelve miles back to my apartment. I didn't want to do all that dead.

"I like going in when I want and not going in when I don't want. That's all. It's got nothing to do with you."

He must have liked that. He grinned and raised his wine glass. "I like a man, does what he wants. Not many of them around no more. Be a shame, taking you out."

"On a date?"

He laughed and slapped me on the shoulder. "No hard feelings, then?"

"Not if you stop trying to make me dead." I raised my glass.

We clinked and drank.

He put his glass down. "Like I said, no need for that. We respect one another, right?"

"Right."

"No reason two fighters like us shouldn't respect one another. That's what's wrong with the world. No one respects one another. Kids running around, shooting other kids, trashing people's homes, getting one another pregnant. Nasty shit. It ain't right. Know what I mean?"

"Kids don't know any better these days."

"I got grandkids myself. I'm from the old school. You treat your elders like royalty. That's how they do it in the old country. My own kids?" He shook his head. "They're imbeciles. *Sfachims*. Don't know when to keep their mouths shut. Now they got kids of their own and theirs are even worse." He poured more wine. "Justice, right?"

"Right."

We clinked glasses again.

He put down his glass and pulled a silver cigar case from his shirt pocket. He offered me one. I took it. He stuck one in his mouth and pocketed the case. Then he pulled a gold monogrammed lighter from his pants pocket and lit our small, hand-rolled, imported cigars. "So then," he said, puffing away, "we tight?"

"Tight," I said. I immediately had trouble holding back a cough. The hot smoke burned my throat. I hated smoking. I hated smelling it and being in the same room with a smoker. It was a major issue when Phil and I lived together. Maybe the wine had relaxed me more than I thought. Or maybe I just didn't want to insult Papa Joe again. He might change his mind about letting me leave here alive.

He blew some smoke toward the woman at the next table. She turned toward us, frowned, and opened her mouth. The man with her kicked her beneath the table. She cringed and glared at him. He whispered something and gestured to Papa Joe with his chin. She shrunk in her chair.

"You work your side of the street and I work mine, then?" Papa Joe said.

"That's kind of impractical, wouldn't you say?"

"Why?"

"You own the street."

He laughed and rapped me between the shoulder blades just I exhaled a small plume of smoke. "You're a good kid, Rafaello."

"Ra-a-a-a-lph," I said, coughing.

"We'll get along."

"I h-hope so."

"Why wouldn't we? I respect you, you respect me. Right?"

I cleared my throat and had some wine. "Just one thing would seal the deal."

"What's that?"

"Brandon."

"Brandon this, Brandon that. All you care about, this punk Brandon."

"I need to find him."

"What the hell for?"

"So I can tell his ex-wife."

"What the hell for?"

"It's my job. It's what I do."

"You *like* going through other people's trash?"

"Like I said, it's what I do."

"What's this Brandon done?"

"He doesn't seem to remember that he has a child."

"Howzat?"

"He hasn't paid his ex-wife child support. She's almost living in the street. She told me she might have to do tricks to feed their kid. She's been living hand-to-mouth for three years. It isn't right, not supporting your own kids." I figured an old-fashioned guy like Papa Joe might appreciate the story better if I embellished it a tad.

"Brandon has a *kid*?"

I nodded.

"Lying *sfachim*." He shook his head. "Never mentioned a kid."

"His ex-wife has the proof. Kid's three, now."

"You're working for her?"

"Yep."

"How's she paying you?"

"I'm doing this for free." My fingers were crossed under the table.

Papa Joe stared at me, then shook his head and blew on the hot end of his cigar. "He ain't paying for his own kids?"

"Not for three years."

"Son of a bitch."

"You can say *that* again."

"That's what's wrong with the world. No responsibility. No self-respect." Raguzzo grunted

279

and poured more wine. "All right. You're a good man. A *stronzone* sometimes, but all good men are *stronzoni*. It's in the blood. But you take the time to help a lady in need and nearly get yourself blown up so she can feed her kid. That's nice. I like that. You got character, Rafaello--"

"Ralph. Thanks."

He sighed. "I'll take care of this for you."

"How?"

"No questions, *Capisc*?"

I knew when to keep my mouth shut. It was enough that he was cooperating. It was also enough that I'd probably still be alive in the morning.

"When can you take care of this?"

"Tomorrow soon enough?"

"Tomorrow's fine." This time I raised my glass first.

Chapter 30

Neil Haversack and a big, dark-haired uniformed cop flanked me in front of the OPD Building at ten o'clock that morning.

Someone had just had a cheeseburger with extra onions, but I didn't want to be rude and ask who it was. I figured the cop. Neil was more of a chicken sandwich kind of guy and a little weird about his weight. Even ate salads regularly. But I didn't say anything. Some cops were a tad sensitive.

Neil said, "What exactly are we waiting for?"

"A deadbeat dad is turning himself in."

"You finally finished that case? And without blowing yourself up?"

"I guess you could say I'm living proof."

He shook his head. "Wonders never cease."

"The world really is a wondrous, never-ending source of amazement." I had the urge to be uncharacteristically philosophical in that moment.

As usual, he ignored me. "Hope this case was worth all the shit."

"He owes three years' worth of child support."

"How much does that translate into?"

"Slightly more than twenty grand."

Neil gave a low whistle. "The courts haven't had a chat with him yet?"

"He's been sort of hiding."

"Where?"

"He's been working for Raguzzo the last several months."

Both Neil and the cop stared at me. Neil said, "And after three years, he's suddenly coming in of his own volition?"

"I had a talk with his boss."

"How'd you manage *that*?"

I shrugged. "Just used my charm."

"Your *what*?"

"Figure of speech."

Neil sighed. "Deacon, from what I've seen the last few days, I'll believe just about anything."

"Papa Joe was the one who arranged our little talk."

"Raguzzo actually *agreed* to let you have one of his boys?"

"He didn't come right out and say this boy works for him."

"But you think he does?"

"I'm almost positive."

"And you managed all this by yourself?"

"Now you've got it."

"How the hell'd you swing this?"

"I made him an offer he couldn't refuse." I didn't even try sounding like Brando. My Brando's horrible.

Neil looked at me as if I'd just unzipped my fly and proceeded to urinate on the street. "And just what was this *offer*?"

"I told him I'd leave him and his organization alone if he complied with my wishes."

"You actually *told* him that?"

"Basically."

The cop was now gawking at me as well.

Neil said, "You realize Raguzzo's nearly a billionaire? Employs more than three hundred people? Owns three dozen businesses? He's been distributing cocaine the last five years and even though we've set up more than eight different sting operations, we can't seem to nail him."

"Yeah, he told me he's pretty successful at what he does."

Neil turned to the cop. The cop looked at him, then at me. They both laughed.

"You're never gonna tell me what really happened, are you?" Neil asked.

"Maybe one day." I saw no reason to lie to Neil. He was my friend. But I also gave my word to Papa Joe. When I give my word, I keep it.

A limo pulled up to the curb across the street. The rear door opened. A tall, broad-shouldered guy around thirty-five took his time getting out. He wore an oversized red sweatshirt, jeans and scuffed white tennis shoes. His hair was shaved down to brown stubble, his cheeks covered with a three-day growth of beard. He'd been punched recently. The bone around his left eye was swollen, the skin itself a bluish green. He didn't take his eyes off the limo as the rear door slammed shut from the inside.

The limo pulled away quickly. He stared at it as if he was a kid being dropped off at reform school.

I walked up to him as he crossed the street. "Brandon?"

"Who wants to know?"

"I'm the guy who's been paid to find you."

He glared at me. He squared his shoulders in an attempt to dwarf me, but for some reason I didn't feel very small at the moment. Actually, I felt pretty damned big. I must've sent over a few vibes because Brandon seemed to deflate a little before my eyes.

"You owe your wife money."

"*Ex*-wife. She's a bitch. A real ball-buster."

"Maybe."

"No maybes. Besides, she lied to me."

"Lied to you how?"

"Said she was on the pill."

"Maybe she was."

"How'd she get knocked up, then?"

"Since you've done this sort of thing before, I really think you're aware of how the process works--"

"You *know* what I mean, goddammit."

I shrugged. "Some women on the pill still get pregnant."

"What good's the fucking pill, then?"

"It works for most."

"Lucky me. She gets knocked up and I'm the one gets the shaft. Typical."

"She's the one paying, so she wins this round."

"What's in it for you?"

"A grand."

"That *all*?" He snorted. "Shit, I make that in a day."

"Also, the knowledge that I'm doing my part to help a child grow up to become as apathetic, angry and as worthless as his parents."

"I shoulda dumped your ass when--" His hands curled into fists. Then he caught himself and bit his lip.

"Was it at Kelsey's? Or Vesper's?"

He didn't speak. His left eyelid twitched.

"We never really got to play our game, did we?"

No response.

"You look kind of naked and helpless without your hammer."

The blood-shot blue eyes bore into me. Brandon really wanted to do me in. Papa Joe probably ordered him to keep his mouth shut and to do whatever he was told. Brandon would have a job when he got out of this unless he did something stupid. That was how hoods acted.

Sometimes the code among crooks made it tough for a good guy to have some quality fun.

Brandon noticed Neil and the other cop. His eyes shot back at me. His body trembled. "If I wasn't being paid a lot of jack to do this," he whispered.

"I know, I know. You really miss your hammer. Maybe they'll give it back to you when you get out."

Neil and the uniform stepped in. They gave Brandon the Miranda read, cuffed him and took him up the walk.

Neil suddenly stopped and turned in my direction. "You coming, too?" he asked.

Actually, I wanted a drink and at least three days of solid sleep. But I also needed to get this wrapped up. Then I wouldn't feel guilty for taking Sandra Brandon's money.

A top-notch private eye is much too busy being respectable to waste his time feeling guilty. About anything.

I followed the threesome up the walk.

Chapter 31

Phil called me the next morning, as I was fixing breakfast.

From the CD player in the living room, Maynard Ferguson played some of the classic recordings he made in the early sixties. The apartment rang with Maynard's high-note trumpet screaming "*Maria*."

"You're still alive," Phil said. It was one of those statements that sounded like a question.

"You had doubts."

"What? I can't hear you. You've got that screechy Canadian trumpet guy playing full-blast, don't you?"

"Maynard's my main man." I turned down the volume, then went back into the kitchen. Using my spatula, I carefully slid the scrambled eggs onto a plate, dropped the toast and the bacon beside the eggs and put my breakfast on the counter. I went out into the dining room and climbed onto one of the three stools I kept under the counter. "You were saying?"

"It's academic now. If you were dead, you wouldn't have answered the phone."

"There'd be no need to if I was dead."

"I take it you've managed to stay out of trouble, then? At least, for now?"

"Of course. No problem."

"Really?"

"There you go, sounding doubtful and nervous again."

"Well, duh."

"You've always shown such confidence in me."

"Can't help it. I lived with you for too long and saw you do some really stupid things."

"I've matured since. Grown. Developed. I'm what you might call seasoned now."

"Okay. . . ." She didn't sound convinced. "So what happened when you left my place? Are those nasty people still looking for you? What did you do about it? Do I still have to worry about them coming after me?"

"So many questions for so early in the morning."

"Ralph . . ."

I nibbled on some bacon, then ate a forkful of scrambled egg. I was *such* a good cook. "Everything's all right."

"By that you mean--"

"Everything's all right."

"You didn't--"

"No."

"And I don't have to--"

"You're fine."

I heard her sigh. "I'm so--"

"I understand."

When you know someone as well as I knew Phil, you don't have to waste time with long, drawn-out conversations.

I drank some coffee and visualized her sitting at the counter in her bathrobe, smoking a cigarette and trying to figure this out. She was probably pushing a hand through her long dark tresses and frowning, trying to decide what part of what I'd told her was true and what part wasn't. She'd think I was kidding or keeping things from her so she wouldn't worry.

I needed to shift the conversation and get her worrying about other things.

"That guy who was there the other night?"

"You mean the other guy?"

I stiffened. "There was more than *one*?"

"*You* were here, silly . . ."

"Oh yes. Now I remember."

"So . . . what about the other guy?"

"Will he be over there again?"

"Why?"

"Just in case I'm in trouble again and have to come over there to hide from bad guys."

"I don't want you doing that again."

"Doing what?"

"Coming over here to hide from bad guys."

"All right."

"Promise me?"

"Promise you what?"

"You won't come over here to hide again."

"I promise."

"Now. What were you saying?"

"The next time I have to go over to your place unexpectedly, I don't want to meet him. It's not that I'm obnoxious or anything."

"Of course not . . ."

"It's just that, well, if I'm in trouble and there are bad guys looking for me, I won't be in the mood to be cordial."

"But you won't be coming over here because bad guys are after you."

"I won't?"

"You just said you wouldn't do that again. You promised."

"You're right. I did. But if I do come over there again, I won't want to be nice to him. I might *try* to, but it won't come out right. He'll know I'm not sincere. So will I. So will you."

"I totally understand."

"It's the principle of the thing."

"Agreed."

"*Do* you?"

"Of course."

"Well, then?"

"Well then, what?"

"If I come over and he's there--"

"He probably won't be."

"Probably?"

"It didn't work out."

"Really?" I was grinning before I even realized it.

"You don't have to sound so *happy* about it."

"How'd you know I'm happy about it?"

"I can hear you grinning."

"You can *what*?"

"I know you, Ralph. I can tell when you're grinning."

"All right. I confess. I *was* grinning. I'm sorry."

"We just didn't click."

"Not like you and me, right?"

"Ralph, be careful, all right? A lot of crazies are out there."

"Really?"

"And stop being so sarcastic and silly."

"I'll try, but it won't be easy."

"I know. And I also know you're still going to do what you're going to do."

"Yes, but things are better now. More fun. Less dangerous."

"What's different?"

"That guy who wanted me dead?"

"The man who tried drugging you?"

"His boss."

"You mean more than one person wants you dead?"

"The guy who drugged me was working for the other guy, who--"

"What about him?"

"He's my buddy now."

She went silent.

"Did you hear me?"

"Ralph, why would a criminal who employs people to hurt, maim or kill other people--why would the same person who wanted you dead want to be your friend now?"

"It's a guy thing. You wouldn't understand."

"Because I'm not a guy?"

"Women can't possibly understand what's going on in a guy's mind."

"We don't have the time."

"For what?"

"To stand around and wait for something significant to happen up there."

"*Touché*. But we *are* buddies now."

"If you say so . . ."

"Things are much better. I've got friends in high places. I've also developed a sixth sense."

"You mean you're still hearing *voices*?"

Couldn't slip anything past this lady. "I can't complain. They've gotten me out of trouble several times."

"Are you *sure* you're all right?"

"Why wouldn't I be?"

"Because you're beginning to sound . . . well, touched."

"Let's just call it intuition."

"And what about your hallucination?"

"You mean the brunette?"

"Of course I mean the brunette."

"You're not jealous, are you?"

"Ralph . . . what about the brunette?"

"She's probably just a female version of my intuition."

Phil went silent again. I couldn't blame her. What could anyone say to something like that?

She finally said, "Are you sure you don't need to have your head injury checked out?"

"It's healing nicely."

"I sincerely hope so. I'm not ready to attend your funeral."

I knew she still loved me. She just didn't want me to get a swelled head. It would irritate my goose egg.

"You're actually *worried* about me?"

"I don't look good in black."

"You look spectacular in black."

"I don't want to have to face your mother. She's still angry with me for divorcing you."

"She's not the only one," I said.

Chapter 32

After breakfast I put Miles Davis's *Sketches of Spain* on the CD player and settled back in my armchair with a fresh cup of Dutch chocolate coffee.

And thought about Mike.

Death is something you only think about when you're sick, facing a major trauma, or attending someone's funeral. It's scary, unpleasant, and depressing. The only time I really thought about death was when I was facing it. I thought about a lot of things when I was zip-tied to that chair in the warehouse behind Vesper's. I thought about turning into Superman, breaking the chair into metal splinters and shoving Mr. Hood's ball-peen hammer right up his ass. I also thought about dying, about how right Phil was about my career choice and how much of an idiot I was to have gotten myself in that predicament.

But mostly about death. I thought about the pain of being tortured, then what would happen later, once Mr. Hood grew tired of his game. What he'd do with my body. Where he'd take it. How he'd dispose of it.

A steady slew of morbid, depressing things.

But not once did I think of what would become of my spirit.

I'd thought about Mike almost constantly in the days following her fall from the balcony. For weeks I wandered around like a zombie, blaming myself for not being there sooner, for not being able to pull her back up, for not being able to hold her until the firefighters arrived and positioned their net beneath her. The case had scarred me--not only because I was new to the field but because I'd been so helpless in the situation. I hated myself for not being able to shoot the pervert before he had the chance to snatch Mike and drag her over to the balcony.

I seldom thought about the fact that I'd almost followed her down. Mike's weight had pulled me over the balcony. I would've gone down as well, had she not let go and fallen to her death. But that wasn't what bothered me. In fact, it took weeks before that fact even drifted back into my drawer of guilt and self-indulgence. My death hadn't even mattered. The cold fact remained: I was unable to save the life of an innocent young woman. Nothing else entered my cluttered brain.

It took months before I finally admitted to myself that her death wasn't my fault.

But no matter whose fault it was, a beautiful young woman named Alicia Freeman was still dead, and it took quite a while before I let myself revert back to being my obnoxious, wise-cracking self.

I still found it hard to believe she'd come back. I couldn't help wondering if my crack to the head was what had caused all this in the first place. Even now I couldn't help wondering if that had really happened or if it was just my quirky imagination taking control all along. If it was my imagination, it certainly had done a remarkable job.

Miles launched into "*Saeta*," one of my favorites on that disc.

"Thinking about me?"

I didn't even have to turn. "Need you ask?"

"Just making sure."

"Don't bother. You've just about taken over every bit of space in my brain."

"I hope that's a good thing."

"It probably is. There was a lot of space up there not being used at all."

"You sure are funny."

"I've heard that before. Once or twice."

She came right over and sat on the couch, facing me. She wore a pink tank top, dark-blue Capri's and stylish black pumps. Her hair was tied in a ponytail. Her eyes were concealed beneath huge, red-tinted sunglasses.

"Spirits need sunglasses?"

She shrugged. "I thought I'd experiment. Women are always trying to look better."

"Even in the Afterlife?"

She shrugged. "Not much else to do."

"You don't need them. Besides, they're hiding your eyes. You've got beautiful eyes."

"You're flirting."

"You're dead."

"You're still flirting."

"I've flirted with married women, single women, engaged women, hookers, strippers, cashiers--you name it. I've even exchanged some heated winks with a blond chick hauling around a sledgehammer at a construction site off Robinson. But never with a dead girl."

"How'd the thing with the blond construction lady go?"

"Never followed through."

"Why not?"

"The sledgehammer turned me off."

"I thought that's what attracted you."

"I was afraid I'd piss her off and she'd use it on me."

She pulled off the glasses and put them on the couch. "Better?"

"Much. They real?"

"As real as I am."

They quickly faded into the upholstery.

"Do you want to know more about Brandon?"

"The case is closed. I no longer care."

"I thought you'd be curious."

"I guess I am. In sort of a half-assed way."

"Why half-assed?"

"I'm more interested in you."

"Let me tell you about him first."

Since she'd saved my life so many times, I decided to let her have her way. I'd learned years ago that things go really smoothly when you let a female have her way. I'd also learned that the situation can get extremely painful and unpleasant when you argue with her. It was probably no different when the female was dead. "Go ahead."

"He was one of Raguzzo's drivers."

"Figured as much."

"Brandon drove one of Raguzzo's vans to Biloxi every week."

"He's got a casino up there, I hear."

"Two, actually. They both had to be replaced after Katrina. They're back, but one block inland. The vans are specially made so the cocaine is easily concealed. They're no different from any other white van you see on the highway--older, beat-up and non-descript."

"Why Brandon?"

"He doesn't look suspicious."

"You mean he's not Arab, Hispanic or black."

"The Interstate cops are on the lookout for certain types. The traffic on I-75 and I-95 is awful, and they can't possibly stop everyone. The cops patrolling I-10 have the same problem. And Raguzzo's drivers are told to stay with the flow."

"Which means they can average ninety and make it to Biloxi in less than seven hours."

"They park in one of the warehouses. Raguzzo's special casino employees unload the van, wash it down, treat it with chemicals, then take it somewhere else and sell it. Brandon is given a different van to return to Orlando. If he's stopped, there's no evidence."

"Brilliant."

"Raguzzo's been doing using this same method for five years."

"And vans are always used?"

"Sometimes SUV's, other times Lincoln Town Cars. Never the same type of vehicle."

"Are the same drivers used?"

"Raguzzo alternates them so the cops can't remember them. Brandon drives most of the time because he's always changing his appearance."

I remembered what Sandra said about her ex always growing something or shaving something off. For a moron, Brandon was smart.

"And since he's not very dark and fairly nondescript, he doesn't stand out," I said.

"Exactly."

"No wonder OPD can't nail Raguzzo."

"He's very shrewd."

"And you found out all this at his mansion?"

"And at Vesper's. You can really get around when no one can see you."

"Shame you're dead. You could be a really great detective."

"But I'd be *seen* . . ."

"Well, yeah."

"Then I couldn't do *any* of this."

"What did you do? When you were alive, I mean."

"Why do you want to know?"

"I'm curious."

"Doesn't matter now, does it?"

"Not at all."

"Why ask, then?"

"I'd like to know more about you. About that day."

"The day I died?"

"It still haunts me."

"What does?"

"Everything. Your being out in the hall when that pervert was getting away. The fact that he was able to drag you to the fire escape. The fact that I couldn't pull you--"

"Stop it." She'd turned away and began watching my CD player as if noticing it for the first time. I could tell I'd upset her.

"I guess you don't want to hear all that again, do you?"

"It won't solve anything. You did your best."

"It wasn't good enough."

"It was enough that you tried."

"My next question is why?"

"Why what?"

"Why all of a sudden did you find me and--"

"Actually, I've been following you around a long time."

"How long?"

"A few years."

"Why haven't I seen you before?"

"I didn't want you to."

"What's different now?"

"You needed help. You were in--"

"Way over my head. Yeah. I got that."

"Answer your question?"

"Does this mean I won't see you again?"

"Not at all."

"When will you pop up again?"

"The next time you're in over your head, silly."

"I don't understand."

"It's simple. You tried saving my life. You couldn't. We bonded just before I died."

"You mean when I was holding onto you?"

"Our spirits kind of meshed together. I've become your angel. Now I'm supposed to return the favor."

"So there actually *is* some order in the universe?"

"You're surprised?"

"Just sort of down on how things are on this side."

"It's not that way where I am now."

"So what do you do when you're not busy saving my ass?"

She shrugged. "Floating around, checking out things."

"Is that what death is? Floating around?"

"So far."

"Met anyone else? Other spirits?"

"I see a few here and there, but I don't usually mingle."

"Why not?"

"I was a loner when I was alive. Why should I be different now?"

"Makes sense. Ever see your folks?"

"Not yet. One day, maybe. Their happy place was Westport, Connecticut. They're probably wandering around somewhere up there."

"*Solea*" started up.

Mike crossed her legs. A real shame she always wore Capri's. She had great calves. My imagination would have to supply the image of how I thought her thighs looked. I could see myself sharing dinner, drinks and my bed with this terrific

301

lady. After all, I'd solved a rough case and got some really bad people off my back. I even managed to stock up on some Jack's and put a few hundred bucks into my starving checking account.

She glanced at the CD player again. "You have anything by *Blood, Sweat, and Tears*?"

"Please . . ."

"Just checking."

"Want to hear them instead of Miles?"

"Miles is fine. I was just wondering. In case I come back for a visit and ask to hear something different."

I tried hard not to stare. I couldn't help it. Her being dead didn't make her any less sexy. A man wasn't terribly particular when a hot-looking woman was concerned. He only cared about a girl who could press his buttons.

"You don't look like a happy camper," she said.

"Does it show that much?"

"What's the problem?"

"You're not real."

"You already know that."

"I know. But when you're dressed like that--"

"What's wrong with the way I dress?"

"Not a *damned* thing."

She sighed. "I'll wear a sheet next time."

"I won't even look at you if you do."

"You *like* being frustrated?"

I shrugged. "I'm a man."

"That's right. Men don't know how to act when they're not frustrated."

I had a sip of coffee, glanced at her legs again and reminded myself they weren't real. It didn't help. Nothing would. So I had another sip of coffee and cursed myself for not spiking it with Jack's.

She stood.

"You're leaving?"

"You don't need me now, do you?"

"You're . . . nice company. And you like my music."

"I'll be back."

"But only when I need you."

"That's the way it works." She crossed the room. "Do me a favor."

"What's that?"

"Don't do anything stupid for a while?"

"When have you ever known me to do anything stupid?"

She just smiled.

"I am what I am," I said.

"What you are is lucky. Most people who do stupid things don't have spirits like me to guide them. Which is why they stay stupid."

"I'll try and remember."

She waved on her way through the front door.

I went into the dining room, parted the drapes, and peered outside.

There was no sign of her.

For the first time in ages, I experienced a heavy sense of loss.

Chapter 33

The following Monday, I drove to my Orange Avenue office a little after eleven in the morning.

I'd spent the weekend hanging around the apartment in my shorts and the personalized white sweatshirt that said *DEACON* in black letters on the front and *COOL ONE* on the back. I needed some time away from the office and decided that the weekend was the perfect opportunity to recharge my batteries. I listened to my Coltrane, Count Basie and Don Ellis CDs, and watched a couple of movies from Netflix. One of them starred Naomi Watts. The movie with Naomi was confusing in spots, boring in others and had a pointless ending, but at least she appeared half-dressed in a couple of scenes. So it wasn't a *total* waste.

I had pizza delivered for the slasher flick I saw on the sci-fi channel Saturday night. It would have been nice if Mike had shown up, but she didn't. When I thought of it a little more, I ended up feeling kind of glad. It would've been awkward, chowing down on pizza with Mike sitting right there, unable to share it with me.

But now that the weekend was over, I wanted to check out my schedule and see if I had anything on my calendar I'd forgotten about. It was clear--at least, for the next couple of weeks. But in this business, a clear schedule means nothing. I could get a call at any given moment from someone needing my services to hunt down an ex or find a wandering teen daughter.

I propped up my feet and got set to try a little blues with my harmonica. I seldom bring it to the office, but since I was still feeling triumphant from the Brandon business, my encounter with Papa Joe and my somewhat eerie reunion with Mike, I decided to indulge myself.

Since I always experience a little sadness between jobs, possibly brought on by boredom, "*Cry Me A River*" immediately came to mind. I also considered "*Summertime*" whenever nostalgia hit me, so I added that to my short list. I didn't feel particularly nostalgic, but I did sense some regret. My recent escape to Phil's apartment reminded me of what Phil and I once had. But that was in the past, and anyway we were still on a friendly basis-- at least, as long as I stopped going over to her place to hide from bad guys.

So why should I feel regretful?

Probably because I was sitting alone in an office, wondering what to play instead of sitting in our old living room, watching Phil parading around in her bra and panties.

I decided to start off with a slow version of "*St. Louis Blues*" and jump right into "*Summertime*" when the mood hit me. I liked "*Summertime*" much better, but "*St. Louis Blues*" was easier to get into, and once you were into it, you could go wherever you wanted from there.

The door opened.

A woman around fifty came in. She was bone-thin, her hair colored in strips of browns and golds--possibly to hide the gray. She wore a tan business suit, a red scarf and carried a red handbag. She had sharp cheekbones and lots of thin, wavy lines around her mouth and eyes. Her teeth were stained. She was probably a smoker.

Her nails were long and a glossy red, matching her handbag. I figured she'd just had them done--possibly to see me. Sometimes my sheer animal magnetism gets around even in a place the size of Central Florida.

I told her to have a seat.

"I'm sorry," she said. "I didn't mean to interrupt."

"Is this business?"

"Well, yes . . ."

"Then you're not interrupting."

She took a seat facing my desk and the heavy reek of cigarettes brushed across my face. I'm really good.

"You're not bad," she said.

"Pardon me?"

"You play well."

"I've been doing it a while."

"My nephew plays the flute."

"Small world."

"He's not as good as you, of course."

"How old is he?"

"Twelve."

I grinned graciously. She seemed all right, but every once in a while you couldn't help wondering

306

how certain people's brains functioned. "Maybe in a year or so," I told her.

"I keep telling him to keep it up. Never give up, right?"

"No, giving up has never been cool."

"When you give up, you have nothing."

"Just a bunch of time on your hands and nothing interesting to do."

"You know, that's very true." She was nodding and staring at me as if I'd just said something really intelligent and profound.

"So . . . how did you hear about me?"

"My husband's cousin. You know Neil Haversack, right?"

"You're related to Neil?"

"Just by marriage."

"So . . . what did he say?"

"Well, it's like this, Mr. Deacon . . . I go to this nail salon--"

"I see that. They do good work."

"They should, at *those* prices."

I wanted to tell her to stop going there if it was too expensive. But as I'd learned from all those years living with Phil, you *never* make suggestions. Women want you to listen to them and smile sympathetically--not solve their problems and make them feel stupid. So I smiled sympathetically and didn't say anything.

"Anyway, this nail lady's having problems with her ex . . ."

"What kind of problems?"

307

"The usual. To make a long story short, they have this daughter, and she's missing."

"And this nail salon lady thinks her ex took her?"

"She's not sure."

"Has she gone to the police?"

"Yes, but Neil found out about it and told me to contact you."

"Me rather than the police? Why?"

"Neil says you're really good. He says you've got a sixth sense about things. People underestimate you because you're not very tough, don't look very bright and act kind of silly all the time. People think you're stupid, so they don't take you seriously."

"That's *so* nice of him to notice." Good ol' Neil.

"And no one thinks you're getting anywhere, but you get things done really fast."

"Neil said all that?"

"It must be true, right? Neil doesn't normally think too much of people. I mean, he's been a cop for twenty years and has seen people at their worst. He just isn't impressed about much anymore. He says mostly everyone's an asshole. Don't you think that's horrible, Mr. Deacon?"

"What? Being a cop for twenty years? Thinking mostly everyone's an asshole? Or not being impressed anymore?"

She chuckled. "Neil also said you're a crackerjack."

308

"One day I'm going to have to thank Neil for all his accolades."

"So you think you might be able to handle this?"

"I'm sure I can check out a few things. Where can I find your friend?"

"That's sort of a problem, too. Sharon . . . well, she's missing. No one's seen her in a while."

"How long is a while?"

"Two days, maybe more."

"What about her work?"

"The salon hasn't heard from her."

"And this isn't like her?"

"Not at all."

"Do you know if someone filed a Missing Persons report?"

"I guess I should've asked, huh?"

"It doesn't matter. I'll find out."

"Neil said you'd be able to find both of them."

"I probably can if I put my mind to it."

"You *must* be good. I mean, if Neil tells me to come to you instead of the cops--"

"The cops have miles and miles of bureaucratic obstacles they have to work around to get anything done. I don't have to worry about stuff like that. I also know a few short cuts that help speed things up. Sometimes it gets me into trouble, but that's part of the business."

"And you've got that sixth sense Neil said."

"Yeah, the sixth sense is what really nails it."

"Really?"

"That, plus good contacts."

309

"Lots of them?"

"You don't need that many if you've got the right ones."

"And I take it you've got the right ones."

"Lady," I said, tucking my harmonica safely into my jacket pocket, "when you've got the right friends, you don't have much to worry about at all."

THE END

ALSO BY DAVID BERARDELLI

THE APPRENTICE
JUST A SIMPLE ERRAND
WORKING FOR A MOB BOSS
LOOKING FOR A DEAD GUY
HUNTING THE TALL BLONDE
FAVOR FOR A FRIEND
THE WAGON DRIVER
DEMON CHASER
DEMON CHASER II
DEMON CHASER III
DEMON CHASER IV
DEMON CHASER V

Titles available through:
Fiction4All